There was a clatter at the back door as the *kinder* came in.

Jessie folded the mending. "I'll go up and get things ready for bed."

When she came downstairs afterward, Timothy was on the floor, showing his *daadi* something about his farm animal set, while Becky cuddled on Caleb's lap.

He smoothed back the strands of hair that had slipped out of Becky's braids, and the tender look on his face told Jessie everything was all right between them now.

Even as she thought it, Caleb's gaze moved to her face with a smiling acknowledgment that her words had helped. Her heart swelled. Perhaps they could be friends one day.

Caleb glanced at the clock. "Time you young ones were in bed."

When she bent over to reach for Timothy, Caleb caught her wrist. She raised startled eyes to his, wondering if he could feel her pulse pounding.

"*Denke,*" he said.

He let go, looked away, and Jessie hurried after the *kinder* who were already scrambling up the stairs. She couldn't let Caleb imagine she had any feelings for him. She just couldn't.

A lifetime spent in rural Pennsylvania and her Pennsylvania Dutch heritage led **Marta Perry** to write about the Plain People who add so much richness to her home state. Marta has seen nearly sixty of her books published, with over six million books in print. She and her husband live in a centuries-old farmhouse in a central Pennsylvania valley. When she's not writing, she's reading, traveling, baking or enjoying her six beautiful grandchildren.

Books by Marta Perry

Love Inspired

Brides of Lost Creek

Second Chance Amish Bride

An Amish Family Christmas:
Heart of Christmas
Amish Christmas Blessings:
The Midwife's Christmas Surprise

Visit the Author Profile page at Harlequin.com for more titles.

Second Chance Amish Bride

Marta Perry

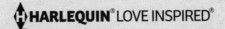

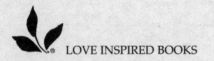

LOVE INSPIRED BOOKS

Recycling programs
for this product may
not exist in your area.

ISBN-13: 978-0-373-62296-2

Second Chance Amish Bride

Copyright © 2017 by Martha Johnson

www.Harlequin.com

Printed in U.S.A.

Do not judge, and you will not be judged. Do not condemn, and you will not be condemned. Forgive, and you will be forgiven.

—*Luke* 6:37

This story is dedicated to my husband, Brian, with much love.

Chapter One

The hospital van bounced over a rut in the farm lane, and Caleb King leaned forward to catch the first glimpse of his home. At last—those four weeks in the rehab hospital after his leg surgery had seemed endless, but finally he was coming back to his central Pennsylvania farm. If only he could jump down from the van, hug his kinder and plunge back into the life of being a dairy farmer.

But he couldn't. His hands tightened on the arms of the wheelchair, and he glared at the cast on his leg. How much longer would he have to count on the kindness of his family and neighbors to keep the farm going?

Caleb glanced toward the Fisher farm across the fields. The spot where the barn had been before the fire was cleared now, and stacks of fresh lumber showed a new barn would soon rise in its place. For an instant he was back in the burning structure with Sam Fisher, struggling to get the last of the stock out before the place was consumed. He heard again Sam's shout, saw the fiery timber falling toward him, tried to dive out of the way…

He should have thought himself blessed it had been only his leg that suffered. And doubly blessed that Sam had hauled him out of there at the risk of his own life.

The van stopped at the back porch. Caleb reached for the door handle and then realized he couldn't get it open. He'd have to wait for the driver to lower the wheelchair to the ground. How long until he'd be able to do the simplest thing for himself? He gritted his teeth. He was tired of being patient. He had to get back to normal.

By the time Caleb reached the ground, Onkel Zeb was waiting with Caleb's two little ones, and his heart leaped at the sight of them. Six-year-old Becky raced toward him, blond braids coming loose from under her kapp, which probably meant Onkel Zeb had fixed her hair.

"Daadi, Daadi, you're home!" She threw herself at him, and he bent forward to catch her and pull her onto his lap, loving the feel of her small arms around him.

"Home to stay," he said, and it was a promise. He hugged her tight. His young ones had lost too much with their mother's desertion and death. They had to know that he was always here for them.

Reminding himself that whatever Alice's sins, he must forgive her, he held out his hand to Timothy, who clung to Onkel Zeb's pant leg. "Komm, Timothy. You know Daadi, ain't so?"

Little Timothy was almost four, and his blue eyes had grown huge at the sight of the lift and the wheelchair. But at the sound of Caleb's voice, he seemed to overcome his shyness. He scrambled into Caleb's lap, managing to kick the heavy cast in the process.

Onkel Zeb winced at the sight. "Careful, Timmy. Daadi's leg…"

Caleb stopped him with a shake of his head. "It's worth it for a big hug from my boy."

Nodding, Onkel Zeb grasped Caleb's shoulder, his faded blue eyes misting over. His lean, weathered face seemed older than it had been before the accident, most likely from worry. "Ach, it's wonderful gut to have you home again."

The driver slammed the van door, smiling at the kinder. "Don't forget, I'll be back to pick you up for your therapy appointment next week." He waved as he rounded the van to go back to the driver's seat.

Caleb grimaced as the van pulled out. "I wish I could forget it. I'd like to be done with hospitals."

"Never mind. You're getting well, ain't so? That's what's important." Zeb started pushing the wheelchair toward the back door, where a new wooden ramp slanted down from the porch. "Sam Fisher and Daniel put the ramp in last week so it'd be all ready when you came home."

"Nice work." Of course it was. His brother Daniel was a skilled carpenter. Caleb tried to look appreciative, but it was hard when he kept seeing reminders of his helplessness everywhere he looked. "Is Sam still helping with the milking?"

"I told him not to come in the morning anymore. With Thomas Schutz working every day, we're getting along all right." Zeb paused. "I was thinking it might be gut to have Thomas stay on full-time even after you're back on your feet. We could use the extra pair of hands."

Caleb shrugged, not willing to make that decision so quickly. Still, Thomas seemed eager to earn the money for his widowed mother, and he was a bright lad. They could do worse than take the boy on until Timothy was of an age to help.

"At least for now we'll keep him full-time," he said. "And we'll have Edith Berger continue with the house and the young ones."

Onkel Zeb stopped pushing when they reached the door. Caleb glanced up and was surprised at the look of discomfort on Zeb's face.

"About Edith…her daughter has been having some health troubles and needs her mamm. So Edith had to go to her. She isn't coming anymore."

Caleb's hands clenched again as the chair bumped over the doorstep into the house. He could hardly care for the kinder when he couldn't even go up the stairs. "We'll have to find someone…"

His words trailed off as they entered the kitchen. A woman in Plain dress stood at the stove, taking a pie from the oven.

"Here's a blessing arrived this morning that we didn't expect." Onkel Zeb sounded as if he forced a note of cheerfulness into his voice. "Look who has komm to help us out."

The woman turned as he spoke. Her soft brown hair was drawn back into a knot under a snowy kapp. She had on a dark green dress with an apron to match that made her hazel eyes look green. The woman wasn't one of the neighbors or someone from the church. It was Jessie Miller, cousin of the wife who'd left him, and the last person he wanted to find in his kitchen.

For a long moment they stared at each other. Jessie's oval face might have been a bit paler than normal, but if she was uncomfortable, she was trying not to show it. Caleb's jaw hardened until it felt it might break. Jessie had offered her assistance once before, just after Alice left, and he'd turned her down in no uncertain terms. What made her think she could expect a wilkom now?

"Caleb." Jessie nodded gravely. "I'm sehr glad to see you home again."

He could hardly say that he was happy to see her, but a warning look from Onkel Zeb reminded him that the kinder were looking on. "Yah, it's wonderful gut to be here." Becky pressed close to the chair, and he put his arm around her. "What are you…how did you get here?" *And why have you komm?*

"Jessie took the bus and got a ride out from town." Zeb sounded determined to fill up the silence with words, probably because he was afraid of what Caleb might say. "It'll be wonderful nice for the kinder to get to know Cousin Jessie, ain't so?"

Caleb frowned at his uncle, unable to agree. He supposed, if he were being fair, that Alice's family deserved some chance to get to know her children, but not now, not like this.

Before he could speak, Zeb had seized the handles of the chair. "I'll show you the room we fixed up for you so you could be on this floor. Becky, you and Timothy give Cousin Jessie a hand with setting the table for supper. Daadi must be hungry, and Onkel Daniel will be in soon."

Becky let go of Caleb reluctantly and went to the drawer for silverware. Timothy raced to get there first, yanking so hard the drawer would have fallen out if Jessie hadn't grabbed it.

"Ach, you're a strong boy," she said, a bit of laughter in the words. "Best let Becky hand you the things, ain't so?" She smiled at Becky, but his daughter just set her lips together and proceeded with the job. Even at her young age, Becky had a mind of her own.

Zeb pushed Caleb's chair to the back room that had been intended as a sewing room for Alice. The hospital bed looked out of place, but Caleb knew it would be easier to get into and out of than a regular bed.

Once they were inside, Caleb reached back to pull the door closed so no one could overhear. He swung to face his uncle.

"What is she doing here?" he demanded.

Onkel Zeb shrugged, spreading his hands wide. "She just showed up. Seems like word got to Ohio about your getting hurt, and Jessie said she thought she was needed."

"Well, she's not." Caleb clamped down on the words. "We'll do fine without her, so she can just take tomorrow's bus right back again."

"Ach, Caleb, you can't do that." His uncle's lean, weathered face grew serious. "Stop and think. What would folks think if you turned your wife's kin out of the house? What would the bishop and ministers say?"

"I don't want her here." He spun the chair to stare, unseeing, out the window. "I don't need any reminders of what Alice did."

"What Alice did, not Jessie," Zeb reminded him. "It's not Jessie's fault. She wants only to help, maybe thinking she can make up a little for what her cousin did."

"She can't." He bit out the words. It was easy telling himself that he had to forgive Alice. It wasn't easy to do it.

"Even so, you'll have to agree to let her stay for a short visit, at least." His uncle pulled the chair back around to give Caleb the look that said he meant business. "I'll not have you hurting the woman for someone else's wrongdoing."

Onkel Zeb hadn't often given orders to Caleb and his brothers, even though he'd shared the raising of them. But when he did, they listened.

Caleb clenched his jaw, but he nodded. "All right. A short visit—that's all. Then Jessie has to go."

With Caleb out of the room, Jessie discovered that she could breathe again. She hadn't realized how hard this would be.

Caleb had changed over the years, just as she had. She'd first seen him on the day he'd met her cousin, and a lot of years had passed since then. His hair and beard were still the color of a russet apple, and his cheeks were ruddy despite his time in the hospital.

But the blue eyes that had once been wide and enthusiastic seemed frosty now, and lines etched their way across his face. Lines of pain, probably, but maybe also of grief and bitterness. Who could wonder at that, after what Alice had put him through?

Guilt grabbed her at the thought of the cousin who had been like her own little sister. She'd been meant to take care of Alice, but she'd failed.

A clatter of plates brought her back to the present

with a jolt, and she hurried to the kinder. "Let me give you a hand with those," she said, reaching for the precarious stack Becky was balancing.

"I can do it myself." Becky jerked the plates away so quickly they almost slid onto the floor. She managed to get them to the round pine table and plopped them down with a clank. "I don't need help." She shot Jessie an unfriendly look.

Had Becky picked up her father's attitude already? Or maybe she saw herself as the mother of the little family now that Alice was gone. Either way, Jessie supposed she'd best take care what she said.

"We can all use a bit of help now and then," she said easily. "I'm not sure where there's a bowl for the chicken pot pie. Can you help me with that?"

Timothy ran to one of the lower cabinets and pulled the door open. "This one," he announced, pointing to a big earthenware bowl. "That's the one for chicken pot pie. Ain't so, Becky?"

He looked for approval to his big sister, and when she nodded, he gave Jessie an engaging grin. "See?"

"I do see. That's just right, Timothy. Do you like chicken pot pie?"

Still smiling, he nodded vigorously. "And cherry pie, too." He glanced toward the pie she'd left cooling on the counter.

Jessie took the bowl, smiling in return at the irresistible little face. Timothy, at least, was friendly. Probably he wasn't old enough to remember much about his mother, so her leaving and her death hadn't affected him as much as Becky.

She began ladling out the fragrant mix of chicken and homemade noodles. The men would doubtless be back and hungry before long. Even as she thought it, Jessie heard the door of Caleb's room open and the murmur of voices.

"Let's get those hands washed for supper," she told Timothy. "I hear Daadi coming." She reached out to turn on the water in the sink, but Becky pushed her way between Jessie and her brother.

"I'll do it." She frowned at Jessie. "He's my little bruder."

Jessie opened her mouth, found herself with nothing to say and closed it again. Her mother's voice trickled into her mind, and she saw again the worried look on her mother's face.

"I wish you wouldn't go. You'll be hurt."

Well, maybe so, but she couldn't let that stop her from doing what was right. She had to atone for the wrongs Alice had done, and if she was hurt in the process, it was probably what she deserved. Given Becky's attitude, she didn't doubt that Alice's daughter was hurting inside, too.

The hustle of getting food on the table was a distraction when Caleb and his uncle returned to the kitchen. Zeb went to the back door and rang the bell on the porch. Almost before its clamor had stilled, Caleb's brother Daniel came in, pausing to slap Caleb on the back.

"So you're home at last. I thought I would have to sneak you out of that hospital."

Caleb's face relaxed into the easygoing smile Jessie remembered from his younger self. "You just want to have more help around here, that's all."

"Can't blame me for that. I've got the carpentry

business to run, remember? I can't spend all my time milking cows."

Daniel's gaze landed on Jessie, and he gave her a slightly quizzical look. He'd already greeted her when she'd arrived, so he wasn't surprised to find her there as Caleb had been. Maybe he was wondering how Caleb had taken her arrival. If so, she didn't doubt he'd soon see the answer to that question.

She'd have known Caleb and Daniel were brothers even if she'd never seen the two of them before. Their lean, rangy bodies and strong faces were quite similar, though Daniel's hair was a bit darker and of course he didn't have a beard, since he'd never married.

That was strange enough to be remarked on in the Amish community. At twenty-eight, Daniel was expected to have started a family of his own. She'd heard from the talkative driver who brought her from the bus station that folks around here said the three King brothers had soured on women because of their mother's desertion. If that were true, she couldn't imagine Alice's actions had helped any.

There was another brother, too, the youngest. But Aaron's name was rarely mentioned, so Alice had told her once. He'd jumped the fence to the Englisch world a few years ago and hadn't been back since as far as she knew. Nothing about the King boys was typical of Amish males, it seemed.

Jessie found herself seated between Zeb and Timothy, and she scanned the table to be sure she hadn't forgotten anything. Silly to be so nervous about the first meal she'd cooked in this house. It wasn't like she was an inexperienced teenager.

Caleb bowed his head for the silent prayer, and everyone followed suit. Jessie began to say the Lord's Prayer, as she usually did, but found her heart yearning for other words.

Please, Lord, let me do Your will here. Give me a chance to make a difference for Alice's children.

For a moment after the prayer, no one spoke. The dishes started to go around the table, and Jessie helped balance the heavy bowl while Timothy scooped up his chicken pot pie. Warmed by his grin, she passed the bowl on to Caleb. He took it with a short nod and turned away.

Zeb cleared his throat. "It looks like you found everything you needed to make supper." He passed the bowl of freshly made applesauce.

"The pantry is well stocked, that's certain sure. Lots of canned goods." She couldn't help the slight question in her tone, since Alice hadn't been here to do the housewife's job of preserving food last summer.

Zeb nodded. "The neighbors have been generous in sharing what they put up. Some of the women even came over and had a canning frolic when the tomatoes and peppers were ready in the garden."

"That was wonderful kind of them." The King family didn't have any female relatives nearby, so naturally the church would pitch in to help. "And someone made this great dried corn. That's a favorite with my little nieces and nephews."

Before anyone could respond, Becky cut in. "You don't have to go back to the hospital anymore, right, Daadi? So we can get along like always."

Zeb's face tightened a little, and he glanced at Caleb as if expecting him to correct Becky for rudeness. But if Caleb caught the look, he ignored it. "I'll have to go for just a few hours each week. It's what they call physical therapy, when they help me do exercises to get my leg working right again."

Becky's lips drew down in a pout that reminded Jessie of her mother. "I thought you were done."

"The therapy will help your daadi get rid of that heavy cast and out of the chair," Daniel said, flicking her cheek with his finger. "You wouldn't want him to skip that, ain't so?"

Becky shrugged. "I guess not. But only for a little while, right?"

It wasn't surprising that Becky wanted reassurance that her father would be home to stay. She'd certainly had enough upheaval in her young life.

"Don't worry," Caleb said. "We'll soon be back to normal. I promise."

Jessie rose to refill the bowl with pot pie. Caleb glanced her way at the movement, and his intent look was like a harsh word. She knew what he meant by *normal*. He meant without her.

By the time the uncomfortable meal was over, Jessie was glad to have the kitchen to herself while she washed the dishes, though a little surprised that Becky didn't insist on taking over that job, too. The little girl certainly seemed determined to convince everyone that Jessie was unnecessary.

Jessie took her time over the cleaning up, half listening to the murmur of voices from the living room. It sounded as if Caleb was playing a board game with the young ones, and Daniel was helping Timothy keep up with his big sister. The play was punctuated now and then by laughter, and the sound warmed Jessie's heart. Obviously everyone was as glad to have Caleb home as he was to be here.

She was just hanging up the dish towels to dry when Daniel and the children came back in the kitchen and started putting on jackets. "Going someplace?" she asked.

Daniel nodded. "These two like to tell the horses good-night. Timothy says it makes the horses sleep better."

"It does," Timothy declared. "Honest."

"I'm sure you're right," Jessie said. "Do you take them a treat?"

"Carrots," he said, running to the bin in the pantry and coming back with a handful.

"Share with Becky," Daniel prompted, and Timothy handed her a few, obviously trying to keep the lion's share.

Jessie had to smile. "Your mammi used to do that when she was your age," she said.

Timothy looked at her with a question in his eyes, but Caleb spoke from the doorway.

"Best get going. It's almost time for bed."

"Komm, schnell. You heard Daadi." Daniel shooed them out, and the door closed behind them.

"Don't talk about their mother to my children." Caleb's voice grated, and he turned the chair toward her with an abrupt shove from his strong hands that sent it surging across the wide floor boards.

For a moment Jessie could do nothing but stare at him. "I only said that—"

His face darkened. "I know what you said, but I

don't want her mentioned. I'm their father, and I will tell them what they need to know about her."

Her thoughts were bursting with objections, but Jessie kept herself from voicing them. "I didn't mean any harm, Caleb. Isn't it better that they hear people speak about Alice naturally?"

The lines in his face deepened, and Jessie felt a pang of regret for the loss of the laughing, open person he'd once been.

"I won't discuss it. You'll have to do as I see fit during your visit."

He'd managed to avoid speaking Alice's name thus far, and that should have been a warning in itself. Arguing would do no good.

"Whatever you say. I'm just here to help in any way I can."

Some of the tension seemed to drain out of Caleb, but not much. She suspected there was more to come, and suspected, too, that she wasn't going to like it.

"Since you're here, you may as well visit with the kinder for a few days." Instead of looking at her, he focused on the National Parks calendar tacked to the kitchen wall. "I'll arrange for you to take the bus back to Ohio on Friday."

"Friday? You mean this Friday? Two days from now?" She hadn't expected this to be easy, but she also hadn't anticipated being turned away so quickly.

Caleb gave a short nod, still not meeting her eyes. He swung the chair away from her as if to dismiss her.

Without thinking, Jessie reached out to stop him, grabbing his arm. His muscles felt like ropes under her hand, and the heat of his skin seared through the cotton of his sleeve. She let go as if she'd touched a hot pan.

"Please, Caleb. I came to help out while you're laid up. Obviously you need a woman here, and your uncle mentioned that the person who had been helping couldn't any longer. Please let me fill in."

A muscle twitched in Caleb's jaw as if he fought to contain himself. "We'll get along fine. We don't need your help."

He sounded like Becky. And arguing with him would do about as much good as arguing with a six-year-old.

Would it help or hurt if she showed him the letter Alice had written a few days before she died, asking Jessie to do what she could for the kinder? While she struggled for an answer, he swung away again and wheeled himself toward the door.

"Friday," he said over his shoulder. "You'll be on Friday's bus."

Chapter Two

Jessie lingered in the kitchen until Daniel and the kinder returned. Becky and Timothy ran straight to the living room, as if they couldn't bear to be parted from their daadi for more than a few minutes. Daniel, with what she thought might have been a sympathetic glance at her, followed them.

She stood, irresolute, watching the red glow in the western sky over the ridge. It turned slowly to pink, fading as dusk crept into the valley. She wasn't used to being surrounded by hills this way. Her area of Ohio was fairly flat—good farmland. These enclosing ridges seemed to cut her off from everything she knew.

Caleb made good use of the land on the valley floor, and his dairy herd of forty head was apparently considered fairly large here. Where the ground started to slope upward toward the ridge, she'd spotted an orchard, with some of the trees already in blossom. Too bad she wouldn't be here to see the fruit begin to form. Caleb would see to that.

She turned abruptly toward the living room. Best

make what use she could of the little time he seemed willing to grant her with the kinder. As she entered, she heard Becky's plaintive voice.

"But isn't Daadi going to help us get ready for bed?" She stood in front of her father's wheelchair, and her look of dismay was echoed by the one on Caleb's face.

"Ach, Becky, you know Daadi won't be able to go upstairs for a bit," Zeb gently chided her. "That's why we fixed up the room downstairs for him."

"I'm sorry." Caleb cupped his daughter's cheek with his hand, his expression so tender it touched Jessie's heart. "You go along now, and come tell me good-night when you're ready."

Timothy was already rubbing his eyes. It had been a big day for a not-quite-four-year-old.

"Komm. I'll help you." When Jessie held out her hand, Timothy took it willingly enough.

But Becky's eyes flashed. "We don't need your help."

The sharp words were so unexpectedly rude coming from an Amish child that for a moment Jessie was stunned. She realized Zeb was frowning at Caleb, while Caleb was studiously avoiding his eyes.

"Becky, I'm ashamed of you to speak so to Cousin Jessie." Zeb had apparently decided that Caleb wasn't going to correct the child. "You go up at once with Cousin Jessie, and don't let me hear you talk in such a way again."

Becky looked rebellious for a moment, but at a nod from her father, she scurried ahead of Jessie and her brother, her cheeks flaming. Jessie, clutching Timmy's hand, hurried after her.

She was quick, but not quite quick enough. Behind her, she heard Zeb's voice.

"Caleb, I should not have had to speak to Becky. It's your job to teach your kinder how to behave."

Caleb's response was an irritable grumble that faded as she reached the top of the stairs.

"That's me and Becky's room," Timothy informed her, pointing. "And that's where Daadi sleeps. Onkel Daniel has that next one."

"Onkel Zeb is sleeping in the little front room," Becky said. "He had to move to make room for you." She shot a defiant look at Jessie.

But Jessie had no intention of responding in kind. Becky must see that rudeness wouldn't drive her away, if that was what the child had in mind. It had been a natural thing in a houseful of men for Zeb to put her into the adjoining daadi haus.

"It was nice of Onkel Zeb to let me use the daadi haus," she said. "He's a kind person, ain't so?"

Becky was forced to nod, and Timothy tugged at Jessie's hand, his sister's rebellion clearly passing over his head. "I'll show you where everything is."

With Timothy's help, Jessie soon figured out how he expected to be gotten ready for bed. She had to smile at his insistence on doing everything exactly the same way as always, according to him. Her brother's kinder were just like that. His wife always said that if they did something once, it immediately became a tradition they mustn't break.

The bathroom was as modern as those in any Englisch house, save for the gas lights. And she'd noticed a battery-powered lantern in the children's bedroom—a sensible solution when a light might be needed quickly. Caleb had done his best to make the farmhouse welcoming for Alice and the kinder, but that hadn't seemed to help Alice's discontent.

Alice had been too young, maybe. Not ready to settle down. She'd thought marriage and the move to Lost Creek, Pennsylvania, would bring excitement. But when life had settled into a normal routine, she hadn't been satisfied.

Jessie had seen her growing unhappiness in her letters. Maybe she'd been impatient with her young cousin, thinking it was time Alice grew up. If she'd been more comforting...

But it was too late for those thoughts. Jessie bent over the sink to help Timothy brush his teeth, but Becky wedged her little body between them to help him instead. *Fair enough*, Jessie told herself. A big sister was expected to look after the younger ones. Maybe if she ignored Becky's animosity, it would fade.

A line from Alice's last letter slid into her mind. *"You were right. I never should have come back here to die. Please, if you love me, try to repair the harm I've done to these precious little ones."*

Jessie's throat tightened. She had begged Alice to stay with her for those final months instead of returning to Caleb. But Alice had been determined, and Jessie hadn't been able to stop questioning her own motives. Whose interests had she had at heart?

Pushing the thought away, she reached over their heads to turn off the water. "All ready? Let's go down and say good-night."

Bare feet slapping on the plank floor, the kinder rushed down the stairs. Following more sedately, she saw them throw themselves at Caleb, and she winced at the kicks his cast took. But he didn't seem to notice.

Caleb cuddled each of them, apparently as reluctant to send them to bed as they were to go. It must have seemed like forever to him since his life had been normal, but she knew him well enough to understand he'd never regret risking injury to help a neighbor. That's who he was, and she admired him even when she was resenting the cool stare he turned on her.

"Go on up to bed now." Caleb helped Timothy slide down from his lap. "Sleep tight."

Smiling, Jessie held out her hands. Once again, Timothy took hers easily, rubbing his eyes with his other hand. But Becky pushed past her to grab Daniel's hand.

"I want Onkel Daniel to tuck me in," she announced.

"Sounds gut," he said, getting up and stretching. "Cousin Jessie and I will see you're all tucked in nice and snug. Ain't so, Cousin Jessie?"

She smiled, grateful that he'd included her. "That we will."

"Let's see how fast we can get upstairs." Daniel snatched up Becky and galloped toward the steps.

"Me, me," Timothy squealed, holding his arms up to Jessie.

Lifting him and hugging him close, she raced up the stairs, and they collapsed on Timothy's bed in a giggling heap. Timothy snuggled against her, seeming eager for a hug, and her heart swelled. If circumstances had been different, he might have been her child.

The unruly thought stuck to her mind like a burr.

She remembered so clearly the day she'd met Caleb. He'd come from Pennsylvania for the wedding of a distant cousin, and she'd been asked to show him around. They'd hit it off at once in a way she'd given up expecting to happen to her.

And he'd felt the same. She was sure of it. That afternoon was surrounded by a golden haze in her memory—the beginning of something lovely. A perfect time—right up to the moment when they'd gone in to supper and Caleb had his first look at Alice. She'd turned from the stove, her cheeks rosy from the heat, strands of cornsilk-yellow hair escaping her kapp to curl around her face, her blue eyes sparkling and full of fun.

Jessie wrenched her thoughts away from that long-ago time. No sense at all in thinking about what might have been. They could only live today, trusting in God's grace, and do their best to make up for past mistakes.

Caleb expected Onkel Zeb to chide him again about Becky's behavior once the others had gone upstairs. His defenses went up at the thought. Becky was his child. It was his responsibility how she behaved.

Unfortunately, that wasn't a very comforting thought. He'd let his own reactions to Jessie's presence influence his daughter's behavior. Besides, Onkel Zeb was as close as a father to him…closer, in some ways, than his own daad had been. It had seemed, after Mamm left, that all the heart had gone out of his father. Onkel Zeb had been the one to step up and fill the role of both parents for him and his brothers.

The unfortunate King men, folks said. Mamm had

left Daad, and then Alice had left him. Onkel Zeb's young bride had died within a year of their marriage. Daniel was definitely not looking for a wife, and as for Aaron—well, who knew what he was doing out in the Englisch world?

He darted a look at his uncle. Onkel Zeb was studying him…patient, just waiting for him to realize himself what should be done.

"Yah, you're right. I'll try to do better with Becky."

"And with Cousin Jessie," Onkel Zeb pointed out. "She is not to blame for Alice's wrongs."

"And Cousin Jessie." He repeated the words dutifully. "At least she's nothing at all like Alice was. She's plain, not pretty and flirty."

"To the *Leit*, plain is gut, remember?" Zeb's lips twitched. "I'd say Jessie has a face that shows who she is…calm, kind, peaceable. Funny that she's never married. It wonders me what the men out in Ohio were thinking to let her get away."

Truth to tell, Caleb wondered, too. If anyone seemed meant to marry and have a flock of kinder to care for, it had been Jessie. His mind flickered briefly to the day they'd met and winced away again. He had no desire to remember that day.

But Onkel Zeb's thoughts had clearly moved on, and he was talking about how things had gone while Caleb was in the hospital.

"…working out fine, that's certain sure. Sam just can't do enough for us, though I keep telling him we're all right. Guess he feels like he wants to repay you, seeing it was his barn where you got hurt."

"That's foolishness, and I'll tell him so myself. As if any of us wouldn't do the same for a neighbor.

Sam's got plenty with his own farm to run. They'd best be getting his new barn up soon, ain't so?"

"Barn raising is set for Saturday." Onkel Zeb grinned. "The buggies have been in and out of Sam and Leah's lane all week with the women helping to clean and get the food ready. Nothing like a barn raising to stir folks up."

Caleb was glad Sam's barn would soon be replaced, but Zeb's words had reminded him of something else. "Maybe Leah would know of someone I can hire to help out with the kinder. What do you think?"

Onkel Zeb shrugged. "Not sure why you want to go looking for someone else when you have family right here eager to do it."

Frustration with his uncle had him clenching his hands on the chair. Before he could frame a response, he heard Daniel and Jessie coming back down the stairs. They seemed to be chuckling together over something, and Caleb felt himself tensing. Irrational or not, he wanted his uncle and brother to share his own feelings about Jessie's arrival.

They came in smiling, which just added to his annoyance. Onkel Zeb glanced at them.

"What funny thing did young Timothy say now?" he asked.

"Ach, it wasn't Timmy at all." Daniel grinned. "Cousin Jessie just didn't agree with my version of the story of the three bears."

Jessie shook her head in mock disapproval. "Even Timothy knew there wasn't a wolf in the story of the three bears. That was the three little pigs."

"Maybe you'd best stick to telling them stories about when you and their daadi were small," Zeb suggested. "And not be confusing the kinder. Or better yet, let Jessie tell the bedtime story."

Caleb could feel his face freeze. Zeb made it sound as if Jessie would be around more than a few nights to tell them stories. She wouldn't.

Jessie seemed to sense the awkwardness of the moment. She turned toward the kitchen. "What about some coffee and another piece of pie?"

"Sounds wonderful gut about now." Onkel Zeb seemed to be answering for all of them.

Caleb almost said he didn't want any. But he caught Jessie's gaze and realized how childish that would sound. So he nodded instead. Jessie's guarded expression relaxed in a smile, and for an instant she looked like the girl he'd spent an afternoon with all those years ago.

It was disconcerting. If he hadn't gone to that wedding, if he hadn't met Jessie and through her met her cousin Alice...what would his life have been then?

Jessie cleared up the plates and cups after their dessert, satisfied that her pie, at least, had met with universal approval. She'd have to take any little encouragement she could get.

Zeb and Daniel had gone to the bedroom to set up a few assistance devices the hospital had sent, leaving her and Caleb alone in the kitchen for the moment. She sent a covert glance toward him.

Caleb had his wheelchair pulled up to the kitchen table, and at the moment he was staring at the cup he still held. She suspected that he didn't even see it. His lean face seemed stripped down to the bone, drawn with fatigue and pain. Today had been a difficult transition for him, but he wouldn't want her to express sympathy.

No man wanted to admit to pain or weakness—she knew that well enough from being raised with six brothers. And clearly Caleb would resent it even more coming from her. The hurt she felt for him, the longing to do something to ease his pain…it would have to stay, unspoken, in her heart.

But the silence was stretching out awkwardly between them. "Becky is…" she began. But the words slipped away when Caleb focused on her.

"What about Becky?" He nearly snapped the words.

That didn't bother her. When folks were hurting, they snapped, like an injured dog would snarl even when you were trying to help it.

"She seems so grown-up for her age. Very helpful, especially with her little bruder."

The words of praise seemed to disarm him. "Yah, she is gut with Timothy. Always has been, especially since…" His lips shut tight then.

Especially since Alice left when he was just an infant. Those were the words he didn't want to say. She could hardly blame him. But if only they could speak plainly about Alice, it might do everyone some good.

"I know how Becky feels. I always felt responsible for Alice after her mamm passed."

Caleb's strong jaw hardened. "I don't want to talk about her. Not now. Not ever. I thought I made that clear."

She wanted to tell him that she understood, but that hiding the pain didn't make it go away. It just let it fester. But she couldn't, because he wouldn't listen. If she had more time…

"I'm sorry. I promise I won't say anything about Alice." *Until the day you're willing to talk.* "But please, think twice about sending me away. The kinder are my own blood, like it or not. I want to care for them, and they need me. You need me."

But she could read the answer in his face already. He spun the wheelchair away, knocking against the table leg in his haste. Impulsively she reached out to catch his arm.

"Please…"

The anger in Caleb's eyes was so fierce she could feel the heat of it. He grabbed her wrist in a hard grip and shoved her hand away from him.

"No." Just one word, but it was enough to send her back a step. "We don't need you. I can take care of my kinder on my own. You'll go on the bus on Friday."

Jessie looked after him, biting her lip. She should have known better than to start her plea by referring to Alice. She'd been trying to show that she understood how Becky felt, but she'd approached him all wrong.

Resolutely she turned to the sink and began washing the plates and cups. If a tear or two dropped in the sudsy water, no one would know.

Caleb might not want to hear it, but she did feel responsible for Alice, just as Becky felt responsible for Timothy. She could only hope and pray Becky never went through what she had.

"You're the older one," her mother had always said. *"You're responsible for little Alice."*

Most of the time she'd managed that fairly well.

But when she'd grown older, she'd sometimes become impatient with Alice always tagging along behind her. She'd been about eleven when it happened, so Alice had been only eight. She'd tagged along as always when Jessie and her friends had been walking home from school.

They'd been giggling, sharing secrets, the way girls did when they were just starting to notice boys. And Alice, always there, always impatient when she wasn't the center of attention, had tried to burst into the conversation. She'd stamped her feet, angry at being rejected, and declared she was going to run away.

Jessie's shame flared, as always, when she thought of her response. *"Go ahead,"* she'd said. *"I won't come after you."*

She hadn't meant it. Everyone knew that. But Alice had run off into the woods that lined the path.

"She'll come back," the other girls had said. And Jessie had agreed. Alice was afraid of the woods. She wouldn't go far. She'd trail along, staying out of sight until they were nearly home, and then jump out at them.

But it hadn't worked out that way. Alice hadn't reappeared. Jessie searched for her, at first annoyed, then angry, then panic-stricken. Alice had vanished.

Jessie still cringed at the memory of telling her parents. They'd formed a search party, neighbors pitching in, combing the woods on either side of the path.

Jessie had followed, weeping, unwilling to stay at the house and yet terrified of what the adults might find. She didn't think she'd been quite so terrified since.

It had been nearly dark when the call went up that Alice had been found. Alice wasn't hurt. They'd found her curled up under a tree, sound asleep.

Alice had clung to Jessie more than ever after that experience. And Jessie hadn't dared let herself grow impatient—not once she'd learned what the cost of that could be. She was responsible for Alice, no matter what.

Jessie tried to wipe away a tear and only succeeded in getting soapsuds in her eye. Blinking, she wiped it with a dish towel. She heard a step behind her.

"Ach, Jessie, don't let my nephew upset you."

She turned, managing to produce a slight smile for Zeb.

Zeb moved a little closer, his weathered face troubled. "You think it would be better to talk more openly about Alice, ain't so?"

She evaded his keen gaze. "Caleb doesn't agree, and they are his kinder."

Zeb didn't speak for a moment. Then he sighed. "Do you know why I was so glad to see you today?"

"Because you are a kind person," she said. "Even Alice…" She stopped. She'd promised not to mention Alice.

"Even Alice liked me, ain't so?" His smile was tinged with sorrow. "This business of not talking about her—Caleb is making a mistake, I think. You can't forgive if you can't be open."

"Some things are harder to forgive than others."

"All the more important to forgive, ain't so?" He patted her shoulder awkwardly. "Don't give up. Promise me you won't."

She didn't know how she'd manage it, but she was

confident in her answer. "I didn't come this far just to turn around and go back home again."

Renewed determination swept through her. It seemed she had one person on her side, at least. And she wasn't going to give up.

Chapter Three

❧

Caleb woke early, disoriented for a moment at not hearing the clatter of carts and trays. He wasn't in the hospital any longer. He was home. Thankfulness swept through him, replaced by frustration the instant he moved and felt the weight of the cast dragging him down.

He was home, and those were the familiar sounds of going out to do the milking. He heard the rumble of Onkel Zeb's and Daniel's voices, and then the thud of the back door closing.

The source of the sound switched, coming through the back window now. Thomas Schutz must have arrived—he was calling a greeting to the others, sounding cheerful despite having walked across the fields in the dark.

Onkel Zeb was right about the lad. They should keep him on, even after Caleb was well enough to take on his own work. That would free Daniel to spend more time with his carpentry business instead of being tied to so many farm chores.

Caleb sat up and leaned to peer out the window.

Still dark, of course, but the flashlight one of them carried sent a circle of light dancing ahead of them. Caleb's hand clenched. He should be out there with them, not lying here in bed, helpless.

Stop thinking that way, he ordered himself. He might not be up to doing the milking or going upstairs to put the kinder to bed, but for sure there were things he could do. The sooner the better.

Using his hands to move the cast, Caleb swung his legs out of bed and sat there for a moment, eyeing the wheelchair with dislike. He didn't have a choice about using it, so he'd have to figure out how to do things with it.

First things first. If he got up and dressed by himself, he'd feel more like a man and less like an invalid. His clothes were not far away, draped on the chair where Onkel Zeb had put them the previous night. That clamp-like gripper on a long handle was obviously intended for just such a situation. Maybe he should have paid more attention to the nurse who'd explained it to him.

Getting dressed was a struggle. He nearly ripped his shirt, and got so tangled in his pants he was blessed not to end up on the floor. But when it was done, and he'd succeeded in transferring himself from the bed to the wheelchair, Caleb felt as triumphant as if he'd milked the entire herd himself.

A few shoves of the wheels took him out to the kitchen. Fortunately Zeb or Daniel had left the light fixture on, since he'd never have been able to reach that. Well, he was here, and a few streaks of light were beginning to make their way over the ridge to the east.

Jessie hadn't appeared from the daadi haus yet.

The small separate house was reached by a covered walkway. It was intended to be a residence for the older generation in the family, leaving the farmhouse itself for the younger family. When he and Alice had married, Onkel Zeb had moved in. Now Jessie was staying there, at least temporarily.

Definitely temporarily. Given how irritable she made him, the sooner she left, the better.

"The kinder need me. You need me." That was more or less what Jessie had flung at him last night. Well, he was about to prove her wrong. He'd get breakfast started on his own. Even if he couldn't go up the stairs, he could still care for his own children.

Oatmeal was always a breakfast favorite. Fortunately, the pot he needed was stored in one of the lower cabinets. Maneuvering around the refrigerator to get the milk was more of a challenge.

Feeling pleased with himself, he poured milk into the pot without spilling a drop. Now for the oatmeal. This would need the gripper, but he'd brought it out of the bedroom with him. Congratulating himself on his foresight, he used it to open the top cupboard door. The oatmeal sat on the second shelf. Maybe he ought to have someone rearrange the kitchen a bit to make the things he'd need more accessible. In the meantime, he could make do with what he had.

Caleb reached with the gripper but found it wavering with the effort of holding it out with the whole length of his arm. A little more... He touched the cylinder of oatmeal, tried to get the prongs open and around it. Not quite... He leaned over the counter, focused on the elusive box, determined to get it down.

He reached, grabbed at it, lost his hold, sent the

oatmeal tipping, spilling down in a shower of flakes. The chair rolled with the imbalance of his body. He tried to stop it, and then he was falling, the floor rushing up to meet him. He landed with an almighty thud that felt as if it shook the house.

For an instant he lay there, stunned. Then, angry with himself, he flattened his palms against the floor and tried to push himself up.

"Wait." A flurry of steps, and Jessie was kneeling next to him, her hand on his arm. "Don't try to move until you're sure you aren't hurt."

The anger with himself turned against her, and he jerked away. "It's not your concern."

"Yah, yah, I know." She sounded, if anything, a little amused. "You are fine. You probably intended to drop down on the floor."

Apparently satisfied that he was okay, she reached across him to turn the chair into position and activate the brake. "Next time you decide to reach too far and overbalance, lock the wheels first."

Much as he hated to admit it to himself, she was right. He'd been so eager to show her he could manage that he'd neglected the simplest precaution. While he was still fumbling for words to admit it, Jessie put her arm around him and braced herself.

"Up we go. Feel behind you for the chair to guide yourself." Her strength surprised him, but no more than her calm reaction to what he'd done.

It took only a moment to settle himself in the chair again. He did a quick assessment and decided he hadn't damaged himself.

Jessie, ignoring him, was already cleaning up the

scattered oats. He had to admit, she was quick and capable, even if she was bossy.

"Aren't you going to say you told me so?" he asked.

She glanced up from her kneeling position on the floor, eyes widening as if startled. Then her lips curled slightly. "I have six brothers, remember? I've dealt with stubborn menfolk before. There's no use telling them."

"I suppose one of them broke his leg, so that makes you an expert."

"Two of the boys, actually." She finished cleaning the oatmeal from the floor and dumped a dustpan full into the trash. "Plus a broken arm or two. And then there was the time Benjy fell from the hayloft and broke both legs." Jessie shook her head. "He got into more trouble than the rest of them put together."

He watched as she started over making the oatmeal. Yah, *capable* was the right word for Jessie. Like Onkel Zeb said, it was surprising no man had snapped her up by now. She was everything an Amish wife and mother should be. Everything Alice hadn't been.

Caleb shoved that thought away, even as he heard voices. The others had finished the milking.

Jessie darted a quick glance at him. "No reason that anyone else needs to know what happened, ain't so?"

He had to force his jaw to unclamp so he could produce a smile. "Denke."

Jessie's face relaxed in an answering grin.

Onkel Zeb came in at that moment—just in time to see them exchanging a smile. He cast a knowing look at Caleb.

Caleb started to swing the chair away, only to be stymied because the lock was on. Still, he didn't have to meet his uncle's gaze. He knew only too well what Zeb was thinking.

All right, so maybe Jessie wasn't as bad as he'd made out. Maybe she was deft and willing and good with children. But he still didn't want to have her around all the time, reminding him of Alice.

Jessie's heart had been in her mouth when she'd heard the crash in the kitchen, knowing Caleb must have fallen. She'd been halfway along the covered walkway, and she'd dashed as fast as she could for the house door. When she'd entered the kitchen…

Well, it had taken all the control she had to put on a calm exterior. Even so, her heart hadn't stopped thumping until he was back in the chair and she could see he was all right.

She set a bowl of oatmeal down in front of him with a little more force than necessary. He was fortunate. Didn't he realize that? He could have ended up back in the hospital again.

A stubborn man like Caleb probably wouldn't admit it, even to himself. Any more than he'd admit that he could use her help. Apparently it would take more than a broken leg to make him willing to have her near him.

She slipped into her chair as Caleb bent his head for the prayer. Then she started the platter of fried scrapple around the table. Timothy took a couple of pieces eagerly, but she noticed that Becky didn't serve herself any until she saw her father frown at her. Obviously Jessie wasn't going to win Becky over easily.

Jessie's heart twisted at the sight of that down-turned little mouth. Becky looked as if she'd been meant by nature to be as sunny a child as Timothy, but life had gotten in the way. If only Jessie could help…but there was no sense thinking that, unless she could change Caleb's mind.

The men were talking about whether or not it was too early to plant corn, all the while consuming vast quantities of food. Jessie had forgotten how much a teenage boy like Thomas could eat. He seemed a little shy, and he was all long legs and arms and gangly build. Tomorrow morning she'd fix more meat, assuming Caleb didn't intend to chase her out even before breakfast.

"Sam says he'll komm on Monday and help get the corn planted," Zeb said. "Told him he didn't need to, but there was no arguing with him."

Jessie noticed Caleb's hand wrapped around his fork. Wrapped? No, *clenched* would be a better word. His knuckles were white, and she guessed that the fork would have quite a bend in the handle when he was done.

Caleb wouldn't believe it, but that was exactly how she felt when he refused to let her help.

Timothy tugged at her sleeve. "Can I have more oatmeal?"

"For sure." She rose quickly, glad there was something she could do, even if it was only dishing up cereal.

"I love oatmeal." Timothy watched her, probably to be sure she was giving her enough. "Especially with brown sugar. Lots of brown sugar," he added hopefully.

"A spoonful of brown sugar," Caleb said firmly, coming out of his annoyance. Jessie met his eyes, smiling, and nodded, adding a heaping spoonful of brown sugar that she hoped would satisfy both of them.

"Shall I stir it in?" she asked, setting the bowl in front of Timothy.

He shook his head vigorously. "I like it to get melty on top." He sent a mischievous glance toward his uncle. "Onkel Daniel does, too."

Daniel laughed. "You caught me. But I'll need lots of energy at the shop today. New customers coming in to talk to me about a job." He looked up at the clock. "Guess I should get on my way."

With Daniel's departure, everyone seemed ready to finish up. Soon they were all scooting away. Left alone with the dishes, Jessie looked after them. She'd think Becky was old enough to be helping with the dishes. Probably her desire to take over didn't extend to the dishes. She'd certain sure been doing that at Becky's age. But she wasn't going to be here long enough to make any changes.

When she'd finished cleaning up the kitchen, Jessie followed the sound of voices to the living room. Becky stood backed up to the wheelchair, a hair brush in her hand. "It's easy, Daadi. Just make two braids, that's all."

Jessie stood watching, oddly affected by the sight of the vulnerable nape of the child's neck. Caleb had managed to part Becky's long, silky hair, and now he clutched one side, looking at it a little helplessly.

Gesturing him to silence, Jessie stepped up beside him and took the clump of hair. For an instant she thought he'd object, but then he grudgingly nodded.

Jessie deftly separately the hair into three strands and began to braid.

Caleb watched the movement of her fingers so intently that she imagined them warming from his gaze. If he were going to be doing this he'd have to learn…but of course he wouldn't. He'd find some other woman to take her place once he'd gotten Jessie out of the way. Maybe he already had someone lined up.

But it couldn't possibly be anyone who'd love these children more than she did. She'd come here loving them already because they were all that was left of Alice. Now she'd begun to love them for themselves… Timothy with his sparkling eyes and sunny smile, Becky with her heart closed off so tightly that she couldn't let go and be a child.

Feeling Becky's silky hair sliding through her fingers took her right back to doing the same for Alice, laughing together as she tried to get her wiggly young cousin to hold still. From the time Alice's mother died, she'd been a part of Jessie's family—the little sister Jessie had always longed for. To help raise Alice's kinder, to have a second chance to do it right this time…that was all she wanted. But with Caleb in opposition, apparently it was too much to ask.

The braiding was done too quickly. She showed Caleb how to do the fastening and then stepped back out of the way while he took his daughter by the shoulders and turned her around. "There you are. All finished."

"Denke, Daadi." Becky threw her arms around his neck in a throttling hug. "I'm wonderful happy you're home."

"Me, too, daughter." He patted her.

The thump of footsteps on the stairs announced Timothy. He jumped down the last two steps and ran into the living room. "I brushed my teeth and made my bed," he announced. "Can I show Cousin Jessie the chickens now?"

"She'll like that," Caleb said solemnly. Then he gave her a slight smile. He turned to Becky. "You go along, too."

For an instant Becky looked rebellious, but then her desire to please her daadi won, and she nodded. Timothy was already tugging at Jessie's hand. Together they went through the kitchen and out the back door.

"The chickens are this way." Timothy pulled her toward the coop. "Reddy is my very own hen. I want to see if she has an egg for me."

"In a minute." She tried to slow him down. "Look. Is that someone coming to see us?"

Jessie pointed across the pasture toward the neighboring farm. A woman and a little boy walked toward them, the boy carrying a basket by the handle. He couldn't have been much more than four or five, and he held it carefully as if mindful of his responsibility.

"It's Jacob and his mammi." Timothy dropped her hand to plunge toward the new arrivals. "Look, Becky." His sister nodded and joined him at a trot.

Jessie stood where she was and waited, unsure. This was obviously the wife of the man who'd been helping so much. It was in their barn that Caleb had been injured, and Jessie had formed the opinion that Leah and Sam were close friends of his. That being the case, she wasn't sure what kind of reception she was likely to get.

Leah and Jacob drew nearer. Caleb's kinder had reached them, and Timothy was chattering away a mile a minute to Jacob, who just kept nodding. Taking a deep breath, Jessie went to meet them.

"You'll be Jessie. Alice's cousin." The woman's smile was cautious. She was thirty-ish, probably about Jessie's age, with a wealth of dark brown hair pulled back under her kapp and a pair of warm brown eyes. "Wilkom."

"Denke." It was nice to be welcomed, even if Leah sounded as though she were reserving judgment. Jessie smiled at the boy. "And this must be Jacob."

The boy nodded, holding out the basket to her. "Shoofly pie," he announced. "For you."

"I wasn't sure what you needed," Leah explained. "But I thought a couple of shoofly pies were always of use."

"They surely are," she replied. "Denke."

A lively controversy had already broken out between Timothy, who wanted Jacob to look for eggs with him, and Becky, who thought he'd rather play ball.

"You should do what your visitor wants," she informed her brother loftily.

"Chickens first," Jacob said. "Then ball."

Jessie couldn't help smiling as the three of them ran off toward the chicken coop. "Jacob is a man of few words, I see."

Leah's face took on a lively, amused look that Jessie suspected was more normal to her than her cautious greeting. "Especially when he's around Timothy. Does that boy ever stop talking to you?"

"Only when he's asleep." She looked after them. "I wish Becky…"

"I know." Leah's voice warmed. "If only Becky would loosen up and talk about things, she'd be better off."

"You see it, too, then. It's not just me."

Leah shook her head, and that quickly, the barriers between them collapsed under the weight of their common concern for the child. "No, it's not just you. She may be worse with you, though, because…" She stopped, flushing.

"Because of my relationship with her mother. I know. I don't blame her."

"Still, she must learn to forgive her mother, or she'll be carrying the burden around with her for the rest of her life."

Leah's insight touched Jessie to the core. "That's what I think, too." Unfortunately, Caleb didn't see it that way.

Leah seemed to measure her with a serious gaze. Finally Leah gave a brisk nod. "Maybe you'll be able to reach her while you're here."

"I won't be here long enough, I'm afraid. Caleb… well, I am leaving tomorrow."

"You mean Caleb is insisting you leave tomorrow, ain't so?" Leah frowned. "I've known Caleb King all my life, so I guess I understand. Everyone knows the King men have always been unfortunate with women. It's turned him sour, I fear."

Jessie stared at her. "I heard something like that

from the driver who brought me out from town, but I wasn't sure whether to believe it."

"They've had a string of unhappy situations with women, that's certain sure," Leah said. "Zeb losing his young wife, and then Caleb's mammi running off and leaving the three young ones. And after what happened with Alice…well, it's not surprising folks think so. Or that it's made Caleb bitter."

She hadn't realized just how deep that belief ran from the way Leah spoke of it. Poor Caleb. She knew full well that his attitude wasn't surprising. She just wished she could make a difference.

Leah was watching her, and Jessie had to say something.

"You are wonderful kind to care so much about your neighbors. I just wish we could get to know each other better."

"Yah, I wish it, too." Leah clasped her hand, smiling. "Maybe you could dig in your heels and refuse to leave. Then what would Caleb do? He couldn't carry you out."

They were still laughing at the image when the kinder came running up to them. "Can we help with the barn raising on Saturday, Leah?" Becky looked more enthusiastic than Jessie had ever seen her. "Please?"

"You'll have to ask your daadi. If he says so, we'd certain sure like to have your help. There's lots you can do." Leah held out her hand to her son. "Now we must be getting home to fix lunch. We'll komm again when we can stay longer." She gave Jessie a warm glance. "I hope you'll be here."

"It was wonderful gut to meet you, anyway. And we appreciate the shoofly pies."

Timothy grabbed the basket handle as they walked away. "Can we have some shoofly pie, Cousin Jessie?"

"I'll help carry it," Becky said. "Let's ask Daadi about the barn raising."

They headed for the house, the basket swinging between them, and Jessie followed, smiling a little. For a moment there, in her enthusiasm for the barn raising, Becky had looked like any happy little girl. Somehow the glance gave Jessie hope. That child existed in Becky, if only she could bring her out.

Caleb sat at the kitchen table with a cup of coffee, looking a little startled at the excitement of the children. They swung the basket onto the edge of the table and rushed at their father.

"Daadi, we saw Leah and Jacob." Timothy rushed the words, wanting to be first.

"Leah says we can go to the barn raising on Saturday if you say it's all right." Becky wasn't far behind. "We'll help."

Caleb seemed to have mixed feelings about the barn raising. Was it the fact that he'd been injured when the old barn burned? Or maybe just the thought that ordinarily, he'd be up on the beams with the rest of the community, making sure the barn was finished for his neighbor?

"Barn raising is for grown-ups. I don't know how you'd help," he said.

"Jacob says he's going to carry water. I could do that." Timothy straightened as if to emphasize how tall he was.

"We could carry the food Cousin Jessie fixes. Leah

said they could find something for us to do." Becky didn't look at Jessie when she said the words, but apparently she didn't mind using her if it meant she'd be allowed to help.

Apparently Caleb hadn't told them she was leaving tomorrow.

She touched their shoulders. "Why don't you give Daadi a minute to think? You go and wash your hands, and I'll cut the shoofly pie."

When they'd stampeded toward the bathroom, she turned back to Caleb. "I guess the young ones don't know I have to leave tomorrow. I'll explain to them."

"You don't have to do that."

She frowned slightly. "You mean you'd rather explain it yourself?"

"No." His voice was gruff. "I mean I've been thinking about you leaving. Maybe I was a bit hasty. If you want to, you can stay. But just until I get back on my feet again. That's all."

It wasn't the most gracious of offers, but she was too relieved to boggle at that. She felt as if an intolerable pressure had been lifted from her heart.

"Denke." Jessie struggled not to let her emotions show in her voice. "I would like that, Caleb."

Her time was still limited, but at least she had been given a chance. A quick prayer of thanks formed in her mind.

Please, dear Father. Show me what to do for these precious children.

Chapter Four

❧

Following the noise late Friday morning, Caleb rolled himself into the kitchen. It had turned into a beehive of activity since breakfast, with racks of cookies cooling while Jessie pushed another pan into the oven. Both Timothy and Becky were intent upon baking projects, Timothy with a dish towel tied around him like an apron. Young Thomas leaned against the counter, seeming right at home with a handful of snickerdoodles.

"What's going on?"

His voice brought all the activity to a halt for an instant. Thomas straightened up, flushing and trying to look as if he didn't have his mouth full of cookies.

Jessie straightened, as well, closing the oven door. She was flushed and smiling, and with her eyes sparkling, she didn't look as plain as he'd thought. "We're baking for the barn raising tomorrow. All those workers need plenty of fuel."

"Look, Daadi." Timothy waved a fistful of dough in the air. "I'm making the little balls, see? When Cousin Jessie bakes them, they'll be snickerdoodles."

Caleb wheeled himself closer to the table. "I see. What's Becky doing?"

"I'm rolling them in cinnamon and sugar." Becky's attention was grabbed by the dough Timothy had in his hand. "That's not how to do it, Timothy. They're supposed to be round. Let me."

Timothy flared up instantly. "This is how I do it. You do your own."

Becky reached out to take the dough from him, but before it could turn into a fight, Jessie was there.

"Becky, can you help me? I need these cookies moved to the cooling tray to make room for the next batch. You're old enough to be careful not to touch the hot pan, I know."

Distracted instantly by the thought of doing something Timothy wasn't allowed to do, Becky abandoned the battle over the shape of Timothy's cookies, and peace reigned.

Thomas seemed to sidle toward the door, and Caleb waved him back. "Stay and help if you want." He pushed his chair through the doorway and out onto the back porch.

The sun's rays warmed his face, and he inhaled the familiar aroma of the farm, overlain by the baking scent coming from the kitchen. He should have been grateful just to be home instead of fretting about all that he couldn't do, but it was hard to be helpless.

Still, if he could manage a little more each day, he'd see progress. He just had to make up his mind to it. The sooner he was back on his feet, the sooner life would return to normal. Without Jessie's disruptive presence.

Hands on the wheels, he rolled himself carefully

down the ramp, pleased when he reached the bottom without incident. He turned toward the barn and spotted Onkel Zeb and his brother coming toward him.

"You're out and rolling!" Daniel exclaimed. "Gut work." He grabbed Caleb's shoulder, his face creasing in pleasure.

Maybe Daniel's pleasure was mixed with relief. If the past weeks had been hard on Caleb, they'd been hard on everyone else, too.

"I had to get out," Caleb said. "If you wander into the kitchen, you might get sucked into helping with all the baking that's going on for tomorrow."

"That doesn't scare me off." Daniel headed for the steps. "I'll talk Jessie into a bag of cookies to take to the shop with me." He waved in the direction of his carpentry shop, located in its own building about twenty yards beyond the barn.

"Don't say I didn't warn you." He turned his attention to his uncle. "Thomas is in there, but he looks like he's doing more eating than helping."

Onkel Zeb shook his head. "I don't know where that boy puts it all. He's as skinny as a rake, and he eats all the time." He put his hand on the chair handle. "Headed for the barn?"

"Seems like a gut jaunt. The doctor said to keep busy."

"He probably also said to be careful not to overdo." Zeb moved as if to push the chair toward the barn.

Caleb tried to turn the wheels on his own, but it was a lot harder than he'd expected on the gravel lane. He gritted his teeth and put more muscle into it. He'd have to try harder. Zeb grasped the handles and pushed, too.

For a moment they didn't speak, but then Onkel Zeb cleared his throat. "Seems like you decided Cousin Jessie can stay."

"For a while," Caleb said quickly. He didn't want any misunderstanding on that score. "Just until I get back on my feet."

"What made you change your mind?"

He couldn't see his uncle's face since he was pushing the chair, but he should have known Zeb would want an explanation. And he didn't have one, not really.

"I got to thinking about what you said. About her being kin to the young ones." He hesitated, remembering how he'd felt when Jessie had interceded to braid Becky's hair and then stepped back to let him take the credit. "I have to admit, she seems to care about them."

"She must, giving up her business to komm all the way from Ohio to help, ain't so?"

Caleb blinked. "Business? What business? I thought she just lived with her brother and his wife."

"She does. She helps out a lot there, too. But she has a business of her own, making baked goods to take to the Amish markets in a couple of towns. Way I hear it, it's turned into quite a success."

Caleb stopped pushing and swung to face his uncle. "How do you know all this?"

"All you have to do is talk to get to know a person." There was a chiding tone to Zeb's voice that made itself heard. He meant that Caleb should have done the same.

Caleb ducked away from the implied criticism. "I guess that's why she looks like she does about all that baking she's doing," he muttered.

"How does she look?"

Caleb shrugged. "I don't know. Happy, I guess." Pretty. Not beautiful, the way Alice had been when they'd met, but appealing in her own way.

"If she's used to baking for market, I guess she'd take a little thing like a barn raising in her stride." Onkel Zeb frowned a little. "As for the barn raising, are you wanting to go over for it?"

Caleb's jaw tightened, and he slapped the chair. "Not likely I can be much help, is it?" Besides, he wasn't sure he wanted to visit the site of his injury so soon. He'd relived the accident enough times already.

But Onkel Zeb's frown had deepened. "Sam's been doing a lot for us while you've been laid up. Seems like it's only neighborly to go over for a spell. Visit with folks, anyway. I was thinking you could use the pony cart. It's low enough that it wouldn't be hard to get in, and the chair could go in the back."

When Caleb didn't answer right away, his uncle shrugged. "Think on it, anyway."

It wasn't easy to hold back when Zeb gave him the look that said he'd be disappointed in Caleb if he didn't go. So he supposed he'd be hauling himself into the pony cart tomorrow.

But as for his uncle's other expectation—well, why should he be interested in finding out more about Jessie's life? She'd be gone soon enough, anyway, and he wouldn't have to think about her at all. That would suit him fine, wouldn't it?

Jessie brought the pony cart up to the bottom of the ramp on Saturday. She'd been wryly amused at the expression on Caleb's face when he'd realized he'd have to let her help him get to Sam and Leah's, since Zeb and Daniel, along with Thomas, had gone as soon as they'd eaten breakfast.

She stopped the black-and-white pony so that the cart was directly in front of Caleb waiting in his wheelchair. Timothy and Becky were on either side of him, Timothy bouncing up and down in excitement.

"Here we are." Jessie hopped out of the cart and scooted around the wheelchair. "I think it will work best if the chair is right next to the cart seat." She moved it into position as she spoke and then set the brake.

Caleb didn't say anything, but he looked as if he held quite a few words back. He reached out for the cart. She intercepted him.

"Better let Becky get up there first, and she can steady the cast and help lift it in. Right, Becky?"

"For sure." She was already scrambling in, eager to help her daadi.

"Me, too." Timothy pouted.

"We need you to hold the chair steady so it doesn't wobble when Daadi pushes off it. You think you can?" Jessie asked.

"Sure. I'm strong." He seized the arm of the wheelchair and planted both feet, gritting his teeth.

"I can swing myself over." Caleb sounded for all the world like his son. He grasped the rail on the cart seat. It was lower than a buggy, but still higher than the wheelchair.

"A little extra help never hurts." Before he could object, Jessie slid her arm around him. "Ready? Go."

She hadn't given him time to argue, but she felt him stiffen, probably not liking her so close.

And they were close, very much so. Caleb grasped

her shoulder with his free hand, his body pressing against hers for what seemed a long moment. Fighting not to react, Jessie concentrated on lifting him. Becky grabbed the cast, and in a moment Caleb was seated in the pony cart, breathing heavily.

She was breathless, too, but not from the exertion. She hadn't expected—well, whatever it was she'd felt when she'd held him against her.

Nothing, she told herself fiercely, and knew it wasn't true. It seemed the feelings that had been aroused that long-ago afternoon were still there, ready to flare up. Maybe that was why her mother feared coming here would hurt her.

While the kinder argued about who was going to sit next to Daadi, Jessie folded the wheelchair and lifted it into the back of the cart. Then she placed the tins of cookies in with it.

"Just hush," Caleb said. "One of you should walk over with Cousin Jessie since there's not room for all in the cart. Who will it be?"

Neither of them wanted to, she thought with a stab of pain. Of course they'd both rather go with Caleb. "It's all right," she began, but before she'd finished, Timothy had hopped down.

"I'll walk with you, Cousin Jessie." He took her hand. Her heart gave a thump at the feel of his small hand put so trustingly in hers. Mamm had been right—being here hurt, and leaving would hurt even more.

But that didn't matter. Nothing mattered except helping Alice's children face life happily again.

Timothy beguiled the short walk by talking about what kind of barn he'd build when he was big enough.

Jessie encouraged him even while she was keeping an eye on the pony cart and hoping Caleb wasn't over-estimating his strength. But the cart arrived safely, and she could see several of the men helping him down and establishing him in the wheelchair. He was probably delighted that he didn't have to rely on her this time.

They had barely reached the fringe of the crowd of helpers when a smiling teenage girl appeared. "I'm helping to look after the kinder. Timothy, why don't you come along so your cousin can help the women with the food?"

Timothy switched over happily enough, spotting his friend Jacob with the other children. Jessie wasn't surprised that the girl knew who she was. Everyone in Lost Creek probably knew it by now. How they felt about it was another matter. Everyone here had known Alice. They had known what she did to her family. Would their attitude toward her carry over to Jessie?

Another teenager had gathered up Becky, and Caleb was surrounded by a group of men, so Jessie headed for the pony cart to get the cookie tins. Leah would probably want them brought to the kitchen, and the sooner she managed to face these people, the better.

The kitchen buzzed with activity. Women un-packed food and tried to put just one more casserole in an already crowded oven. Jessie hesitated inside the screen door, searching for Leah, and spotted her wedging a dish onto the refrigerator shelf.

Jessie made her way to Leah, aware of furtive glances from the other women. "Leah?"

Leah turned, her face warming with a smile even

though she looked as distracted as any homemaker would who had a few too many people in her kitchen. "Jessie, I'm wonderful glad you came. Did Caleb make it, as well?"

Jessie nodded. "He used the pony cart. Easier to get into with his cast."

"Gut, gut. He'll be wanting to be outside after all that time in the hospital." Leah glanced around as a pan clattered in the sink.

"You're busy," Jessie said quickly. "Where do you want these tins? They're snickerdoodles and whoopie pies."

Leah looked for an available flat surface and didn't find one. "Let's put them in the pantry for now." She led the way. "My shelves are getting empty now that the winter is over."

The pantry still looked very well stocked with Leah's canning, but Jessie found an empty shelf and slid the tins onto it. "Is there something I can do to help?"

Leah rolled her eyes. "Everyone asks that, but just now, I need to get organized. Once it's nearly time to serve the men, I'll need everyone's hands. Until then…"

"You'd prefer our space to our presence," Jessie said, smiling. "I understand. I'll be back."

When she returned to the kitchen, she saw that most of the other women, having deposited their offerings, were scattering outside. Leah would have organized some reliable workers, probably kinfolk, to be her aides, and they'd work best without interference. Jessie was too used to the routine of this sort of work frolic to have any doubts.

Outside, Jessie paused on the back porch to get her bearings. Long tables, probably the same ones that would be turned into benches for worship on Sunday, were already set up, and the teenage girls had the young ones corralled a safe distance from the barn going up. She caught a glimpse of Becky and Timothy chasing around with other kinder in some sort of game.

The barn was already taking shape, as the men had been hard at work since dawn. They swarmed over it like so many purposeful bees, each worker knowing the task assigned to him. Sam and Leah must be sehr happy to see their whole community contributing to their new barn. She could well remember the day the new barn had gone up on her brother's farm—he hadn't been able to stop smiling all day.

Jessie searched for Caleb almost without planning it. His wheelchair was placed next to a long wooden table that held supplies the workers would need. Even from here, she could see the tension in his figure— the way his hands gripped the arms of the chair as if he'd propel himself out of it. Watching the work go on without him must have made him feel more helpless than ever. Maybe it would have been best…

"Don't worry too much about Caleb." The unexpected voice came from behind her, and Jessie swung around to see an older woman watching her with sympathy in her face. "There, my husband is talking to him. Josiah will keep him from fretting."

Jessie suspected her cheeks were red. "I didn't… I mean…"

"Ach, I know." The woman patted her arm. "I'm Ida. Ida Fisher, Sam's mother." She gestured toward the addition to the farmhouse. "We moved into the daadi haus a few years back to give Leah and Sam's family more space. And you are Alice's cousin, komm all the way from Ohio to help out."

Jessie nodded cautiously. This woman, at least, didn't seem to harbor ill will toward her because of Alice. "I arrived on Wednesday."

"I know," she said again, chuckling this time. "The Amish grapevine works wonderful fast here in Lost Creek. Are you finding your way around all right?"

"It's fine. Onkel Zeb is a big help. And Timothy isn't shy about telling me how things should be done."

"He's a talker, that one. Such a sweet child. He and our little Jacob are growing up gut friends, just like his daadi and Caleb always were. So you don't need to worry that Caleb will get into mischief trying to help. Josiah is looking out for him, and Sam will, too. The two of them have taken care of each other more times than I can count—even when the barn was burning."

"That was when Caleb was hurt, ain't so?" She'd heard only a brief reference to the accident since she'd been here.

"The Lord was watching over both of them that day, that's certain sure." Ida's blue eyes misted with tears. "They were getting the animals out when they saw a burning timber coming toward them, Sam says. Caleb jumped, but it came down right on his leg."

Jessie touched Ida's arm in quick sympathy. "I'd guess Sam got him out, ain't so?"

Ida nodded, blotting the tears away with her fingers. "Yah, he did. I'm being foolish, crying when they're both safe. But that's how those two boys always were, getting into trouble together and pulling each other out."

"Caleb's fortunate to have such gut friends and neighbors to help him, especially since Alice…" Jessie stopped, not really wanting to talk about Alice with someone she hardly knew.

"Poor Alice." Ida shook her head. "The way I see it, she's paid for whatever mistakes she made. It's way past time for forgiveness."

Jessie's throat was tight. "I wish everyone felt that way."

Ida studied her face as if searching for answers. Whatever she saw seemed to satisfy her, because she gave a short nod.

"Maybe your visit will help. Make Caleb and the rest of the community face what they're feeling. The gut Lord forgives us in the same measure that we forgive others. That should give all of us pause, ain't so?"

Jessie nodded, and Ida gave her hand a little pat. "I see Josiah has gone off to check on something. Maybe a gut time for you to see if Caleb needs anything."

Was that a hint? If so, maybe she'd best follow it. Sam's mother seemed the kind of wise woman her own mother was, who always saw beneath the surface of other folks.

At least Ida was ready to be friendly, as was Leah. Perhaps Jessie's acceptance here wouldn't be so difficult after all.

She stopped a step or two short of Caleb's chair. He hadn't noticed her, probably because his gaze was intent on the workers busy erecting the framing for the barn's loft. Well, she couldn't just stand here.

"They're working quickly." A foolish comment, but at least it drew Caleb's attention.

He glanced at her and then gave a short nod. Impossible to tell what he was thinking when he wore that stern expression.

"It's going to be a bit larger than the last one, according to Sam," he said just when she thought he wasn't going to speak. "He's been impatient to get it up."

Jessie's tension eased. At least he was talking to her. Maybe she could distract him from thinking that he ought to be up there, balancing on a beam, hammer in hand.

"Close to a month they've been waiting, so Onkel Zeb says. No wonder he's eager to see it done."

"Yah, he says it was one thing after another—first delays at the sawmill, then bad weather, then Elias Stoltzfus down with the flu."

"Elias Stoltzfus?" Stoltzfus was a common enough name among the Pennsylvania Amish, but she hadn't heard of him since she'd been here.

"He's planned every barn in Lost Creek in the last forty years. No one would think it right to start building without him. Especially Elias." There was the faintest twinkle in Caleb's eye.

"I see. Moses Miller is the barn planner out in our community. If he doesn't walk it out first, no one will start to build." In fact, folks were starting to wonder what would happen when Moses, already eighty-four, couldn't go on.

Caleb glanced at her in a way that was almost friendly. "Guess there are as many things the same out in Ohio as there are different."

"I guess so. I keep expecting to see bicycles, but I gather that's not part of your tradition."

Caleb shrugged. "I've heard tell bicycles are allowed out in the Ohio communities because folks tend to live farther apart."

That hadn't occurred to Jessie before, but maybe it was the reason. There certainly seemed to be a big concentration of Amish farms along this road, whereas in Ohio, they'd more likely be interrupted by Englisch homes.

"Probably that's why." She saw that he was staring at the men working the very top of the barn. "I suppose you're one of those who likes to work up top."

He actually chuckled at that. "I guess. The first time I was a bit scared, but when I got up there, it felt pretty good. And Sam... Sam was never afraid of heights. He was climbing to the top of the big oak tree when he wasn't much more than Timothy's age."

"Better not let Timothy hear you saying that, or we'll be coaxing him down, ain't so?"

"You've noticed he's a bit sure of himself."

"You could say that." Relief bubbled up in Jessie that they were actually talking together as though they were kin, maybe even friends.

"He's always been that way. Crawling out of his crib at ten months, he was." Caleb's smiling gaze met hers—met and held for a long, breathless moment.

They both looked away, and Jessie prayed that color wasn't flooding her cheeks. "Well, I...I came over to ask if there is anything you need."

"No. Nothing." Caleb grabbed a box of nails from the table next to him and began counting them as if the success of the barn raising depended on knowing how many nails were used.

"I'll go along and help with the lunch, then."

Jessie went hurriedly toward the house, imagining she felt people looking at her. Watching her every move with critical eyes.

Nonsense. Folks had better things to do than to think about her. Some teenagers put plates and napkins on the tables, and women were starting to head into the kitchen. She'd be needed to help carry things out.

They'd feed the workers first, of course. That was always how it was done. That way the builders could have a bit of a break to let their food digest before getting back at it. If it was like most barn raisings, they wouldn't want to leave today until the barn was under roof, if not completely ready to use.

After the men had eaten, the women and children would take their turn at the tables, enjoying the plentiful food. Always enough and more—that was the Amish table. And then there'd be all the cleaning up to do.

She searched for Timothy and spotted him still running, maybe a little slower than before. The boy had plenty of energy, but he was likely to tire out before too long. That might be a good excuse to get Caleb to go home, as well. He'd been out of the hospital only a few days, and he'd probably been told to take it easy, although he wouldn't want to admit it.

Taking a deep breath, she prepared to plunge into the maelstrom of activity in the kitchen. All of the other women seemed to have the same idea, but the service was surprisingly orderly. Each person picked up a dish handed over by Leah or one of her helpers and then filed out with it, passing those still waiting in line.

With the assembly line working at full speed, it wouldn't take long to have everything out to be served. Jessie's thoughts fled back to Caleb. He might need someone to help the wheelchair across the grass. But of course one of the men would assist him. He didn't need her.

Jessie grabbed the dish of whipped potatoes that was handed to her and hurried back out the door, following the lead of the woman ahead of her in placing her dish. Then she started back, not sure whether there would be a second round of deliveries.

The entry line seemed to have slowed to a crawl, so Jessie stopped on the porch. A glance back told her that the men were already taking their places on the long benches, and she spotted Caleb with his wheelchair situated at the end of one table. So that was all right.

She tore her attention away from him in time to hear the conversation of the women ahead of her, who were just inside the screen door.

"…terrible, having the nerve to come here and move in on Caleb after what her cousin did. I'm surprised Caleb let her stay."

Jessie was frozen in place, cold hands clasping one another.

"Caleb had better watch out, that's all," the other woman said. Jessie caught just a glimpse of her when she moved—an older woman, sharp-featured, wearing black. "A helpless widower with two young children… She's out to trap him, that's what. Did you see her watching him? Not content with her cousin breaking his heart…now she's after him herself."

Jessie took a step back, then another. She had never been so mortified in her life. How could anyone possibly think that about her?

Well, she'd wondered how she'd be accepted here, hadn't she? Now she knew.

Chapter Five

Caleb didn't want to admit how much the barn raising had taxed his strength, but by Sunday morning he had no choice but to face it. He wasn't the person he'd been before the accident, and there were days he feared he never would be.

He tried to shake off the feeling as he struggled into the wheelchair. That process was getting easier, he reminded himself. The doctors had been right to insist he spend two weeks in the rehab hospital. Without that time, he wouldn't have been ready to come home.

Now for today's challenge—going to worship. This was church Sunday, and folks would expect to see him there. Their community, like most in Pennsylvania, held worship every other Sunday. He wheeled himself out to the kitchen.

Jessie was already at the stove while Onkel Zeb, Daniel and the kinder sat at the table eating. Jessie's smile looked a little strained as she spooned up oatmeal for him and poured a mug of coffee.

Now that he thought about it, she'd seemed unusually quiet after they'd returned home from the barn raising yesterday. He gave a mental shrug. He didn't understand what made Jessie tick, and that was just fine. He'd been pushed by circumstance into accepting her help, but that didn't mean he wanted to be friends.

Daniel gave him a sidelong look as he took his place at the table. "You sure you should be going to worship today? Nobody would blame you if you stayed home."

He glared at his brother. "I'm fine." He bit out the words. Daniel shrugged, not impressed by his ill humor. Or maybe thinking it showed he wasn't fine at all.

"I want to be at church," he added, modifying his tone so nobody could accuse him of being cranky. "I've missed it. Anyway, that's where we belong on a church Sunday, ain't so?"

"That's certain sure." Jessie put a bowl of scrambled eggs on the table and then took her seat. "I suppose a lot of the folks who were at the barn raising were from your church district?" Her tone made it a question.

"Most of them," Onkel Zeb said. "Some were from the next district over. Here, each bishop has two districts. Is it that way out in Ohio?"

Jessie nodded, her mind seeming to be on something else. Whatever it was, it had taken the sparkle from her eyes.

Caleb frowned. But he worried how he would manage just getting to worship. He didn't need to be wondering about Jessie.

Daniel and Onkel Zeb had obviously given some

thought to the problem of transporting him to worship. They'd rigged an improvised ramp to lift him to the level at which he could move over to the buggy seat. He and Daniel would go in the smaller buggy, while Onkel Zeb took Jessie and the kinder in the family buggy.

He barely suppressed a sigh once he was settled on the buggy seat. Daniel picked up the lines and released the brake before he spoke. "I don't want to get my head bitten off, but don't push yourself too hard."

Caleb pushed down the frustration that wanted to release. "Sorry," he muttered. "I hate seeing everyone else carrying my load."

"Guess I'd feel that way, too," Daniel admitted. "But you'd do the same for every one of us, ain't so?"

Caleb grunted. "It's easier to be on the giving end."

His brother grinned. "Maybe the gut Lord decided to teach you some humility."

Was that true? If so, the Lord had surely found the hardest way of doing it—forcing him to depend on Jessie, of all people. The idea was enough for him to chew on the rest of the short ride to the Stoltz farm, and he still hadn't finished with it when they arrived.

Daniel took the buggy right up to where folks were gathering outside the barn—men and boys arranging themselves in one line while women and girls did the same in another. Soon they'd be filing into the Stoltz barn for worship, going from oldest to youngest, as always.

Several men hurried forward to help, and Caleb was lifted down and installed in the wheelchair almost before he had time to brace himself. Becky and

Timothy came running over, trailed by Onkel Zeb and Jessie.

Funny. He took another look. Jessie's strained expression seemed to have intensified. Was it possible she was nervous about meeting all these people who were as close to him as family?

"I'll sit by you, Daadi." Timothy grabbed the arm of the wheelchair, bouncing up and down.

"No." Becky's pout had returned. "I want to sit next to Daadi."

"You'll sit on the women's side, like you always do," Onkel Zeb said firmly.

"No, please, Daadi. I want to sit with you."

Jessie didn't speak. She just looked at him, and Caleb knew she was waiting for his verdict. But there couldn't be any question, could there?

"Becky, you always sit on the women's side. Go with Cousin Jessie now."

Jessie held out her hand, smiling at his daughter. "Komm. I need you to show me where to go in the line."

Becky folded her arms mutinously, and Caleb's patience snapped. "Rebecca Jane, stoppe! Go to your cousin this instant!"

He'd spoken so sharply that several people nearby turned to look at him. Becky's lips trembled. Annoyed with her and disgusted with himself, he spun the chair away.

What kind of father was he turning into? What was wrong with him?

"Komm." Jessie's voice was soft, but it reached him, and he felt sure she'd taken Becky's hand. "Folks are cross when they're in pain, ain't so? We just have to understand and love them, anyway."

If it was possible for him to feel any more ashamed than he did already, Jessie's words would have done it.

Jessie breathed a silent prayer that Becky would understand. Then Becky took her hand and led her toward the lineup of women and girls. As they passed the single young women, Becky hesitated, glancing up at Jessie.

Jessie answered the question in the child's face. "At home I sit with the women who are about my age, even though they're all married but me." Becky obviously hadn't known where to put her, which wasn't surprising. Everyone from her rumspringa group was long since married, and it had seemed foolish to sit with younger and younger unmarried girls. She had no plans to be married, so the day she'd joined them had been a silent announcement, if any were needed, that she considered herself a spinster.

Not a pretty term, but it was true. She'd given up the idea of marriage a long time ago.

Now the question was how to avoid the women she'd heard talking about her yesterday at the barn raising. She cringed inside at the memory of those hurtful words. *Forget them*, she ordered herself, but since she'd been saying the same thing all night, the command didn't seem to be working.

She'd had only a quick glimpse of one face, so how would she know them for sure? And for all she knew, everyone here was thinking the same thing, even if they weren't so outspoken about it.

Fortunately, before Jessie could sink any deeper,

she saw Leah gesturing to her. Relief lifted her heart. She had one friend here, at least. That was something to thank the gut Lord for.

Leah greeted her with a smile. "Komm, sit with us."

"Denke." Leah couldn't know how thankful she really was. "Becky is showing me around this morning."

"Gut." Leah touched Becky's cheek lightly. "I'm glad you're taking care of your cousin. And everyone will be sehr happy to see your daadi back in worship this morning."

Becky nodded without speaking, still looking on the edge of tears. Jessie could almost believe the child pressed a little closer to her. Maybe it was possible to break through the barriers Becky had put up between them, but she certain sure didn't want it to be at the cost of Becky's close relationship with her daadi. This was proving much trickier than she had imagined when she'd left home so full of hope.

The line started to move then, so there was no time for more. But Becky's hand stayed in hers all the way into the barn and while they filed into the rows of benches on the women's side of worship.

The two rows of mammis and small children were so placed that they had the rumspringa-age girls in front of them and then the row of young girls who were deemed old enough to sit together in worship. Their older sisters and mothers would keep a close eye on them. Jessie smiled a little, remembering the day her brother's oldest had begun to giggle in worship and been escorted, face flaming, back to sit with her mamm.

Sitting on the hard backless benches for three

hours could be a challenge. Jessie let her gaze slide covertly to the men's side, where she saw with relief that Caleb was in his wheelchair, pulled up to the end of a bench next to his brother and little Timothy. At least he hadn't stubbornly insisted on moving to the bench, where his cast would have had little or no support.

"I hope Caleb is not overdoing it." Leah had mastered the gift of whispering just loudly enough to be heard by her neighbor.

Jessie nodded. "Me, too. But he's…" She let that trail off, not wanting to seem critical.

"Stubborn." Leah supplied the word, the corner of her mouth twitching. "I know."

The song leader began the long, slow notes of the first song, with the rest of the worshippers joining in. Jessie had no need to consult the book of hymns to join in the familiar words. Next to her, Becky sat very straight, adding her small voice to the song of praise.

Jessie was relieved that the service was familiar from her own church district. There were always differences in custom from one district to another, but from what she had seen so far, Caleb's was very similar to hers in Ohio except for some minor differences in what technology they accepted.

Had that made Alice feel at home when she came here? Or would she have felt stifled by it, with her longing for change and adventure unmet?

Jessie discovered her fingers were twisting together in her lap, and she forced them to be still. Everyone had been happy when Caleb started courting Alice. Apparently Jessie had been the only one to question whether Alice was actually ready for marriage. If she had spoken out then, might it have made a difference?

But she hadn't. She'd been hamstrung by the undeniable fact that she had thought she would be the one Caleb wanted. Anyone might think she was speaking out of her own disappointment.

Jessie didn't think other people's opinions would have stopped her, if only she hadn't feared in her own heart that it might be true that she felt jealous.

Probably the result would still have been the same. *Accept*, the faith counseled. *Accept what God sends as His will.* She'd tried. She was still trying.

Halfway through the long sermon, given today by the bishop, Becky began to sag. Leah eased her arm around the child, wishing with all her heart that Becky would relax against her and accept the love she had to share.

The bishop was talking now of the love the shepherd had shown, leaving the ninety-nine behind to seek and save the one who was lost. Love for his people seemed to shine in Bishop Thomas's face as he spoke, and Jessie warmed to him. She felt for a moment as if he talked directly to her. She wasn't exactly lost, but she was alone in a strange place. Maybe Bishop Thomas was someone she could turn to if necessary.

Becky jerked upright when Leah's two-year-old, Miriam, kicked her legs fretfully as she sat on her mamm's lap. As if it were catching, Becky began kicking her feet.

Jessie pulled her attention away from the bishop's preaching on the lost sheep and exchanged looks with Leah. Both of them were obviously familiar with the efforts involved in keeping small children quiet during a long worship service. And Jessie couldn't help wondering how many people were watching her with critical eyes, ready to seize on the slightest mistake on her part.

Drawing out a white handkerchief, Jessie began shaping it into, if you used considerable imagination, a bunny. She slipped it over her fingers and made it hop over to Becky. Her attention captured, Becky made the bunny hop along her own lap.

Little Miriam made a grab for it and was thwarted by her mother. Smiling, Leah hushed her small daughter and passed another handkerchief over to Jessie so that she could produce a second bunny. In two minutes the kinder were happily…and silently…playing. Peace reigned until the end of worship.

As they rose from the final prayer, Leah turned to her, smiling. "That was a lifesaver, Jessie. You must show me how to do it."

"For sure. But they fall apart pretty fast, I'm afraid."

Becky was tugging at her, so she moved out of the way of the men and boys who were rapidly changing the benches into the tables that would be used for lunch. Later they'd be loaded onto the church buggy, ready to be taken to the next host residence for worship.

Leah was saying something about her fretful daughter when Jessie's attention was drawn away by a voice that was only too familiar. An older woman, filing out of a seat a few rows behind her, spoke to the woman next to her. The words didn't matter, but the voice…the voice was that of the woman who'd said those hurtful words yesterday at the barn raising. When Jessie looked closer, she recognized the sharp-featured face.

Jessie waited a moment before turning to Leah. "Who is the woman just going out two rows behind us?"

"The one in the black dress with the gray hair? That's Ethel Braun. Bishop Thomas Braun's wife."

Jessie's heart sank to her shoes. The bishop had preached about love and forgiveness, and she'd been drawn to him, eased by his words. All the while his wife spread hateful rumors about Jessie. It didn't look as if she could expect any understanding from the bishop.

Why does it matter what anyone else thinks? Jessie, sitting in the living room rocker with a stack of mending that evening, tried to dismiss the reactions of Caleb's community from her mind. She had made a friend in Leah, and some of the other young married women had cautiously approached her, so the prospect of being accepted wasn't entirely bleak. Besides, her job here was to make things better for Caleb and the kinder, not to worry about her own popularity or lack of it.

How Alice had expected her to do that was another question. The last letter from Alice had laid a burden on her, but not even Alice had suggested how Jessie might make things right with the family she'd left behind. Alice probably hadn't known—she'd just had a glimmer of hope that her older cousin would solve her problems, as Jessie so often had.

Jessie picked up one of Becky's dresses from the mending basket. The hem had pulled out—a simple enough fix, but it made her wonder who had been taking care of the mending and sewing for the family. Neighbors or relatives, she supposed, but if so, they'd allowed it to pile up fairly high. She'd have several evenings' work just to catch up.

Caleb cleared his throat, and she glanced at him. He'd seemed engrossed in the newspaper, so she'd respected his silence. But now he was frowning, glancing first at her and then down at his hands.

"About Becky…" He came to a stop, frown deepening.

"What about her?" Jessie kept her voice even, wondering if this would be another warning about what she should or shouldn't say to his daughter.

"I heard what you told her this morning. After I was so short with her."

"I'm sorry if I spoke out of turn." She swallowed a number of things she would have liked to say.

"It's not that." He looked directly at her, and she was startled by the pain in his face. "You were right in what you said. Becky shouldn't question doing what she's told, but there was no reason for me to tell her so harshly."

What could she say? He was right, of course, and yet she understood. "Being sick or in pain does make a person a bit short-tempered."

"It's important that Becky listen." He seemed to be arguing with himself. "But I…I wonder if I should say anything to her about it. If I should…"

"Apologize?" she finished for him. Jessie made several stitches in the hem to give herself time to think. "It's a hard decision. But I remember a time when my daad and one of my brothers were at odds most of the time." Her lips curved upward, remembering. "Joshua was fourteen, and thought he knew all the answers about everything. He got sassy with Daad at a time when Daad was worried about the milk tank leaking. He was afraid we were going to lose a whole day's production and maybe risk the contract with the dairy. Anybody smart wouldn't have butted in at a time like that."

"Joshua wasn't smart, I take it." Caleb's interest had been caught.

"Not as smart as he thought he was, anyway. Josh was the last straw, and Daadi blew up at him." She paused. "He was sorry afterward, that was certain sure. He'd always been fair, and it was like he'd let himself down, as well as Josh."

"Yah, it does feel that way." Caleb ran his hand through his hair in a frustrated gesture. "What did he do about it?"

"At first I didn't think either of them was willing to be the first to speak. But then Daad said he was sorry, that he shouldn't have taken his worries out on Josh. Josh just stood there for a minute. Then a couple of tears spilled over, and the next thing he was crying and saying it was his fault." She grinned. "Which it was, but he finally grew out of being so obnoxious."

Caleb's smile flickered. "Yah, I have little brothers, too. Denke, Jessie."

For once it seemed they were really communicating, without all the barriers between them. Something that had been tied up in knots inside Jessie began to ease.

There was a clatter at the back door as Onkel Zeb, Daniel and the kinder came in from doing the evening chores. Not that the little ones would be much help, as small as they were, but that was how children learned—by standing beside an adult, first watching, then helping, then finally doing it all by themselves.

Jessie folded the mending. "I'll go up and get things ready for bed."

They'd fallen into a routine already in the few days she'd been there. By disappearing upstairs to prepare for the kinder's bedtime, she gave Caleb a few minutes alone with them. He'd need it tonight if he intended to tell Becky he was sorry for his anger.

Jessie understood his hesitation. It wasn't easy to admit you'd been wrong, especially when the other person had been wrong, as well. Caleb wouldn't want Becky to get the idea that it was all right for her to disobey, but he wanted to be honest with her, too.

Taking her time, Jessie got everything ready. Then she started downstairs quietly, ready to retreat if it seemed Caleb was still having a private talk with Becky. But when she reached the spot from which she could look into the living room, all seemed fine. Timothy was on the floor, showing his daadi something about his farm animal set, while Becky cuddled on Caleb's lap.

Relieved at the sight, she went on to the living room, smiling. "This looks like a happy group."

"I was showing Daadi the brown-and-white cow I have. I named her Brownie. Do you think that's a gut name for a cow?" Timothy's blue eyes were very serious.

"Very gut. It describes her, doesn't it?"

He gave a decided nod, and she suppressed a grin at his determination.

"If I had a cow, I'd name her Buttercup," Becky said, leaning against her daadi's shoulder. "Do you think I could have a calf to raise all by myself, Daadi?"

"In a year or so," Caleb said. He smoothed back the strands of blond hair that had slipped out of her braids, and the tender look on his face told Jessie everything was all right between them now.

Even as she thought it, Caleb's gaze moved to her face with a smiling acknowledgment that her words had helped. Her heart swelled. They seemed to have reached a truce, and that was surely enough to be going on with. Perhaps they could even be friends one day.

Caleb glanced at the clock. "Time you young ones were in bed. Put the farm set away now, Timothy."

For an instant Timothy pretended not to hear. Jessie knelt next to him. "Should Brownie go into the barn for the night?" She "walked" the cow toward the barn.

"I'll do it," Timothy said, his smile instantly restored. He set about putting the pieces away, and in a moment Becky slid down from her daadi's lap.

"I'll help."

Jessie stood, smiling. That sort of cooperation was sweet to see between sister and brother. In a normal Amish family, there might be another baby or two by now, and they'd be sharing time and attention, but for Becky and Timothy, there was no other sibling. Or cousin, either, for that matter, and Daniel showed no sign of getting serious about anyone. Maybe he, like everyone else, believed the King brothers to be unfortunate in love.

She waited while Becky and Timothy kissed their

daadi. When she bent over to detach Timothy, who had a tendency to use Caleb's cast to climb on, Caleb caught her wrist. She raised startled eyes to his, wondering if he could feel her pulse pounding.

"Denke," he said again, softly.

He let go, looked away, and time moved on at its usual pace. But for a moment, it seemed to have stopped indefinitely.

The kinder were already scrambling up the stairs, and Jessie hurried after them with more speed than dignity. She couldn't let Caleb imagine she had any feelings for him. She just couldn't.

Timothy was already at the bathroom sink, brushing his teeth, but Becky lingered in the bedroom.

"Cousin Jesse, could I have my hair in one braid for the night? So it won't get tangled?"

"For sure." She tried to keep her elation from filling her voice. Becky was actually letting her do something. This was a red-letter day indeed.

They sat side by side on the bed while Jessie unpinned the silky soft hair and ran the brush through it, careful of any tangles. As she started winding the strands into the loose braid that would be comfortable for sleeping, Jessie found herself slipping backward in time.

Wasn't it just yesterday that she'd done the same thing for Alice? She'd been so glad to have a small girl cousin, since Mamm and Daadi hadn't provided her with any sisters. Alice had been a pleasant change from the boys, who never wanted to sit still for a minute and certain sure wouldn't let her brush their hair.

"There we go."

The bottom of the braid was well below Becky's shoulder blades, and Jessie rested her hand against the child's back as she found the band to secure the braid. How small and fragile Becky seemed in this quiet moment, with the vulnerability of her nape exposed. Jessie was swept with an intense wave of protectiveness.

After Jessie fastened the band, Becky shook her head so that the single braid swung from side to side. "Feels gut."

"Your mammi used to say that, too. You look very like her." The words were out before Jessie remembered that she wasn't supposed to mention Alice to the kinder.

But she didn't have time to worry about that, because Becky's reaction was too violent to let her think of anything else.

"I'm not! I'm not like her!" Becky burst into a storm of weeping and threw herself onto the bed, her whole body shaking.

For an instant Jessie froze, aghast at the reaction to her simple words. Fortunately it seemed no one else had heard. At least, no one came hurrying to see what was wrong.

She bent over Becky, almost afraid to speak for fear of saying the wrong thing again. "I'm sorry, Becky. I didn't mean to upset you. Please forgive me." She kept her voice soft and gentle, praying silently for guidance.

Oh, Lord, help me know what to do for this troubled child.

Becky's sobs eased. "I don't look like her. Not one

little bit." Her voice had returned nearly to normal, interrupted only by a little hiccup.

"If you say so." Jessie hesitated, wondering how much she dared to say. "Is it bad to look like her?" She carefully didn't speak Alice's name.

Sniffing a little, Becky sat up, nodding. For an instant, Jessie thought that was all she'd get by way of explanation. Then Becky blinked away the tears. She stared down at the floor.

"Daadi might not like me if I look like her," she whispered.

Jessie felt as if Becky had grabbed her heart and squeezed it. She couldn't seem to get her breath. How could the poor child have come up with this idea?

But she knew how, didn't she? Caleb, and his determination never to speak of Alice.

She focused on Becky, praying she might feel the love in Jessie's heart. "Your daadi loves you and Timothy more than anything in the whole world, no matter what you look like. I promise you."

Becky pierced her with an intent stare. "Are you sure?"

"I'm sure," she said. "If you were purple with blue-and-white stripes, your daadi would still love you just the same."

That brought the smile she'd hoped for to Becky's face. But it didn't solve the problem.

Caleb should be made to know and understand the harm his attitude was doing to Becky. If Jessie tried to tell him, though, he would turn on her with all the anger bottled up in his heart. The brief truce between them would be over.

He wouldn't listen to her words. But somehow he had to be made to see the truth.

Please, Lord. I don't think I can do this. Please, help me.

Chapter Six

Getting ready for the visiting therapist to arrive on Monday morning, Caleb found he was still a bit uneasy about Jessie. The plan was to have the therapist come every week, while he went to the clinic periodically. Not that it was any concern of his, but she was, in a sense, his guest, and she'd seemed distracted, almost worried, since they'd come home from worship on Sunday.

Even now, while she cleaned up the kitchen after breakfast, Jessie acted as if she was preoccupied with something other than the job in front of her. Maybe she was bored. The thought slid into his mind. After all, Alice had become bored with this life quickly enough.

That was probably unfair. Jessie had spent many years as an adult helping with her brother's children and doing all the things any Amish woman would take for granted. She wouldn't have expected anything else here.

But at the moment he'd rather think she was bored,

illogical as it was, than assume he was in some way responsible for her feelings. He hadn't invited her here.

That justification didn't seem sensible, even to him.

The sound of a car pulling up next to the house put an end to his fruitless imaginings. "That'll be the therapist," he said.

Jessie swung around as if she hadn't realized he was in the room. "Ach, yah, that's who it will be." She dried her hands on a dish towel. "I'll get the door."

The kinder came stampeding down the hall at the sound of the vehicle. "We'll go," Becky said. "We'll get it, Cousin Jessie."

Jessie smiled and nodded, but she followed them. Just as well, since even Becky didn't have much Englisch yet. In September, when she started first grade, she'd begin learning the Englisch an Amish person needed to get along in the world. But around the house and with other Amish folks, Pennsylvania Dutch was spoken.

Becky pulled the door open almost before the man had finished knocking, but then, as Caleb had expected, she was struck dumb with shyness, stepping back and blushing. Thankfully Jessie had reached them by then.

"Please, komm in. Caleb is expecting you."

"I'm Joe Riley." He was young, with reddish hair and freckles, and he grinned at the kinder in a friendly way. "Who are you?"

"This is Becky, and this is Timothy." Jessie touched them lightly as she said their names, and then she switched from Englisch to Pennsylvania Dutch. "Give the gentleman room. He's here to help Daadi with his exercises."

Still speechless, the children backed into the kitchen from the entryway.

The therapist raised his eyebrows at Jessie. "And you are?"

"Cousin Jessie," she said. "Caleb is here." She ushered him into the kitchen, and Joe came over to shake hands with Caleb.

"We met before you were released from rehab, didn't we? I bet you're enjoying being back in your own house after all that time in the hospital. And having some good home cooking, too, right?"

Caleb nodded, wondering why all the therapists he'd run across were so unwaveringly cheerful. "Yah, that's so. It's good of you to come to the house."

"That's my job." Joe set a duffel bag on the table. "We can't just let you sit in that chair when you get home. Have to help you build up your strength so this leg won't be as weak when the cast comes off."

"Yah, I know." Caleb took himself to task for sounding unwelcoming. The man was here to help him, and the more Caleb worked at it, the faster he'd get back to doing the things he wanted.

"Just remember that the leg will be wasted some after all this time in a cast. Even after it comes off, you'll still have to work on getting the strength back in it."

Maybe the therapist thought he needed the cautionary words. He probably did, since he'd seen the cast as the enemy.

"Where would be the best place to work?" Caleb asked.

Joe looked around. "This would be a good spot. Nice smooth floor and not much to trip on. If it's okay to move the table and chairs, that is." He glanced at Jessie as if rearranging the kitchen was up to her.

"Yah, it's fine," Caleb said. This was his house, not Jessie's.

"I'll take the chairs into the dining room." Jessie suited action to words and the kinder, catching on even though Joe had spoken in Englisch, hurried to help.

It was quickly done, and then Joe grabbed one end of the table while Jessie took the other. They put it against the far wall.

"Great! Now we can get to work." Joe was relentlessly happy, and Caleb expected he'd be relentless about pushing him, as well.

"The children and I will get out of your way." Jessie shooed the children gently toward the other room. "Just call if you need anything."

They began with some of the simple routines he'd done in the rehab hospital. After a few minutes Joe called a halt.

"Okay, obviously I don't need to start with building upper body strength. I guess a farmer already has plenty of that, not like somebody who sits at a desk all day."

Caleb hadn't expected to find this process amusing, but he was returning Joe's grin. "Yah, when you're tossing hay bales around, you build up a few muscles."

"Let's get on to the hard stuff, then." Joe bent to check the cast and the pulse in Caleb's ankle. "See, what happens is that this leg is losing muscle all the time it's in the cast. Right?" He glanced at Caleb's face to make sure he was following. "So we want to keep the muscles working as much as possible. That's going to help you move around more easily with the cast on, and also keep you from losing too much. Okay?"

He always seemed to want agreement with his statements, so Caleb nodded. Maybe that was the therapist's way of ensuring that his patient was on board.

"I want to get back to my regular work," Caleb said, "so whatever you say to do, I'll do it. I'm needed here, and I can't run a dairy farm from a wheelchair."

"You might be surprised at what people can do from a wheelchair," Joe said, his face serious. "I worked with a farmer up north of here who couldn't get around without a chair, and he did all right. He even rigged up a lift he could work himself to get from the chair to his tractor."

Maybe Joe meant that to be encouraging, but Caleb didn't care to picture that kind of a life for himself. He would get his strength back, and everything would be as it had been.

"All right," Caleb said. "Let's get to work."

Caleb almost regretted his words over the next half hour. Joe worked him every bit as hard as he'd expected, and Caleb felt convinced that the cast was getting heavier with every repetition.

By the time Joe stepped back with a satisfied nod, he was breathing about as hard as Caleb was. He stood for a moment and seemed to be considering something.

"I'm going to give you a bunch of exercises to do on the days I don't come." He pulled a couple of printed sheets from his bag. "But they're not things you can easily do on your own. What we really need is someone to help."

Before Caleb could respond, Joe had spun and walked into the living room. "Hey, Jessie? Could you come and give us a hand?"

"For sure."

Caleb's jaw tightened at Jessie's quick assent. If Joe expected him to accept Jessie's help with the exercises, he was mistaken.

Jessie and Joe came back to the kitchen, the kinder trailing along behind, their eyes round with curiosity. "Caleb will have to do this routine on the days I don't come, and it's not something the client can do alone. Can I count on you to help?"

Jessie's face didn't give anything away, but Caleb thought she didn't like the idea. Still, she'd never say so. He knew she'd consider it her duty.

Jessie answered as he'd expected. "I'm wonderful glad to help any way I can. What do you want me to do?"

Caleb had to stop this before it went any further. "Jessie has enough to do with the kinder and the house. I can work on my own."

"Sorry." Joe's smile flashed, but he sounded firm. "You really can't. Not and do what needs to be done. This definitely requires another person."

"Then my uncle can help," Caleb said impatiently.

"Is that the older man I saw working outside when I came in? Looks like he already has plenty to keep him busy."

"He does," Jessie said. "I'm the logical person to help Caleb." She turned to the children and spoke quickly without giving him time to argue. "You'll help me with Daadi's exercises, ain't so?"

"We'll help. We'll do a gut job, Daadi. We really will." Becky was solemn in her assurances, and Timothy ran over to scramble up into his lap.

"Looks like you're outvoted," Joe said. He gestured with the papers to Jessie. "Here are diagrams that show exactly how the exercises are supposed to be done. I'll demonstrate them to you, just to be sure."

Jessie nodded, her head bending over the papers. Her soft brown hair was parted in the center and swept smoothly back under her kapp, and the column of her neck was slim and strong. There was determination in the firm line of her jaw. If Jessie thought she was going to give Caleb orders...

But was that really what bothered him about this idea? Or was it the fact that he wasn't sure how he felt about working so closely with her?

"I want to help plant the garden!" Timothy ran alongside Jessie that afternoon, while Becky trailed behind.

"For sure you're going to help," Jessie assured him. "And Becky, too."

Becky's face gave her feelings away so readily. She wanted to participate, and yet she was resentful of each new chore Jessie took over. "Onkel Zeb planted the garden last year," she pointed out.

"He'd like to do it this year, but he's been wonderful busy since your daadi got hurt, so I said we'd help." Jessie glanced at Becky. "He got it all ready for us, and he said you were a big help last year."

Becky's face brightened. "I was. And I'm bigger this year, so I can do even more."

"We'll make a gut job of it, then, with such gardeners." They'd reached the plot not far from the kitchen that had been plowed and harrowed. "Onkel Zeb says we should wait a week or two for the tomatoes and peppers, but we can already plant a lot of the vegetables."

Using the corner of a hoe, she marked out a furrow for each of the kinder and gave each one a seed packet. "Drop just a seed or two at a time," she cautioned, remembering her small nephew planting by the handful.

But these two seemed happy enough to follow directions. Jessie moved along with them. "Not too deep," she cautioned when Timothy poked a hole with his finger. "Remember, when the seed sprouts, it has to work its way clear up through the soil so it can reach toward the sun."

"How long will it take?" Timothy eyed the seeds he'd just planted. "I want to see it sprout."

"Some seeds take a week. Some take two or even longer." Thinking of her nephew's activities, she added, "You can't dig it up to see if it's sprouting, you know. If you do that, it will never grow."

Timothy's mouth turned down. "But I want to see it."

"You will," she assured him. "When it's ready, it will pop up through the ground. A couple of little leaves will start to open. Then you can watch it grow bigger every day."

"Then we'll water it," Becky added. "That will help it grow."

"Yah, that's so." Jessie smoothed the soil over a few more seeds. "Jesus said that our faith is like a tiny seed planted inside us. He helps it grow just like the sun helps the plant grow, until it's strong and healthy and able to do good things."

She wasn't sure Timothy was getting it, but Becky seemed to mull over her words. "Good things like helping other people," she said finally. "Onkel Zeb says a good deed is like a lighted candle in a dark room. It helps folks see."

"Onkel Zeb is a wise man," Jessie said, relieved. She had wondered who was teaching them the gentle examples of faith from everyday life that an Amish mother imparted without even thinking about it. It sounded as if Zeb had sensed that need in Becky and Timothy and was trying to fill the gap.

They'd reached the end of the third row of planting when Timothy leaped up. "Daadi's coming out!" He charged toward the porch, closely followed by Becky, their feet making small prints on the row of newly planted seeds.

Jessie got up slowly. She and Caleb hadn't spoken to each other since the physical therapist left, and she hesitated to bring up the subject. Clearly Caleb hadn't wanted her to be the one to assist him, and she hadn't really wanted to, either.

But she felt quite sure that their reasons were very different. Caleb didn't want to be beholden to her because he resented her presence—or maybe more accurately, he resented the fact that she was a reminder of Alice.

Her reasons were much more complicated. Over the years, she'd convinced herself that she couldn't be blamed for having feelings that had started before Caleb had even so much as seen Alice. And anyway, those feelings had long since faded to the vanishing point.

Unfortunately, she wasn't quite as sure of that fact as she had been. And being close to him, helping him with his exercises, touching him…that could be very dangerous to her emotions. To her heart, which still seemed vulnerable where Caleb was concerned.

The kinder were helping Caleb down the ramp in the wheelchair. Or at least, he was letting them believe they were helping him, which amounted to the same thing in making them feel useful. Her mother always said that a useful child was a happy child, and Jessie agreed. It seemed to her that the worst thing a parent could do was to do everything for a child.

She watched as they approached the garden, Becky very intent and serious as she pushed the chair and Timothy holding on to the arm to ease it along. This opportunity to be with Alice's kinder and help them might be as close as she ever got to parenthood, and she was determined to do it well.

She still had her many nieces and nephews, she reminded herself. But each of them had two parents, and none of them had Becky and Timothy's desperate need.

The chair came to a halt at the edge of the plowed earth. "Look, Daadi." Timothy darted along the row. "I planted all these seeds. They'll grow into carrots."

"We put the seed packet on a stick at the end of each row so you can tell what's planted there." Becky tapped the one closest to her. "They're like little flags, ain't so?"

Caleb nodded and then glanced at Jessie. "Zeb usually takes care of the garden. You didn't have to do it."

He sounded like his daughter, resisting any change in the order of things.

"Zeb has plenty on his hands right now," Jessie said lightly. "He was happy to let us take over the planting. Besides, I love planting the garden. At home, my nieces and I always take care of the vegetable patch and the flowers."

Caleb's hands tightened on the arms of the chair. "Yah, you're right. Onkel Zeb is taking on too much for a man his age."

"Better not let him hear you say that about him," Jessie said lightly, hoping to distract him.

But Caleb just glared at the cast. "I'd like to take a saw to this thing."

A quick glance assured Jessie that the children were at the far end of the garden, out of earshot. "Then you'd never get back to the way you were, ain't so?" Could he feel her sympathy? "It's wonderful hard to be patient."

"It is." His hands eased as if he'd needed someone to recognize how difficult this was for him. "Where's Zeb now? Do you know?"

"In the barn. He said something about fixing a few weak stall boards." She made her tone casual. "Maybe he could use someone to help hold the boards."

Caleb's smile flickered briefly. "Trying to make me feel useful, Jessie? I've seen you do that with the kinder, distracting them from being quarrelsome."

She couldn't help laughing. "I was just remembering something my mamm always says...that a useful child is a happy child."

Surprisingly enough, he took that well. "Maybe grown-ups aren't so different." He raised his voice. "Becky! Timothy! Komm help me out to the barn."

The kinder ran down the lane between the rows. "I'll push," Becky declared, getting there first.

"No, I will." Timothy's face puckered.

"You are both needed to push," Caleb said. "The chair doesn't go so well on the rough ground."

"We can do it," Becky said. She made space for her brother, and they both began to shove.

Jessie hurried to keep pace with them, suspecting another hand might be needed to get up the incline to the barn door. Caleb rolled the wheels with his hands. He must be tired after this morning's hard workout, but he didn't show it.

Caleb darted a quick look at her, and then his gaze dropped. "You never told me about your business out in Ohio."

It took a moment for Jessie to process the unexpected words. Finally she shrugged. "There didn't seem to be a reason to."

"Or an opportunity?"

She shook her head slightly, but it was probably true. They hadn't had many casual conversations, and she tended to pick her words carefully with him.

"Zeb told me about it. He said you gave it up to come and help us."

"I couldn't be there and here, could I? It seemed more important to be here."

"Why?" His eyes met hers, challenging. "Why was this important to you?"

Jessie hesitated. She glanced at the kinder, but they didn't seem to be paying any attention to the adults' conversation. "I grew up being responsible for...for my little cousin."

She wouldn't say the name, afraid of provoking an explosion, and as it was, she was dangerously close. Still, Caleb was the one who'd forced the question.

"I guess I still feel responsible. If I can do something to right a wrong, then I want to do it. I need to do it."

Jessie couldn't bring herself to look at his face, afraid of what she'd read there. He reached out suddenly to grab her wrist, covering her hand on the chair, and her breath caught.

"You aren't..." he began.

But she wasn't to know what he might have said. Becky gave the chair a big shove. "We can take it the rest of the way. We don't need any help."

Jessie let go and watched the children struggle to get the chair into the barn. She wanted to assist, but not at the cost of upsetting Becky.

What had brought on that sudden reaction on the child's part? The fact that Caleb had been momentarily occupied with Jessie? She wasn't sure. But each time she took a step forward with Becky, it seemed to be followed by a plunge backward.

As for where she stood with Caleb...she didn't even want to think about that problem.

Caleb grasped the wheels, helping propel the chair onto the barn floor. It began to roll faster once it hit the worn wooden floor boards.

"Stop pushing now or you'll send me right into Beauty's stall."

For some reason, the kinder seemed to find that

hilarious, and they scampered into the barn, giggling. Jessie followed a few paces behind. It took a moment for his eyes to adjust to the dimness after the bright sunshine outside.

He'd wanted to say something to Jessie, but clearly now was not the time, not with Zeb and the kinder around. Later, maybe. Or was it best to leave the whole subject alone? She couldn't atone for what Alice had done, if that was what she'd meant. Nobody could.

"Ach, you've made it all the way to the barn." Beaming, Onkel Zeb rose from squatting by a stall door. "Looks like you had some helpers."

"Yah, I did." He rolled the chair toward the stall. "Now it's my turn to help. I can reach the stall bars from the chair, anyway."

Zeb gave Jessie a questioning look as if wanting reassurance that he could manage. Caleb tried not to let it annoy him. Onkel Zeb was only acting out of love.

Whatever Zeb saw on Jessie's face must have satisfied him, because he nodded. "I could use an extra pair of hands, that's certain sure."

Becky darted forward to join them. "I'll help, too."

"You already have a job," Caleb said firmly. "That garden isn't going to plant itself. We're counting on you."

He saw the faintest suggestion of a pout forming on his daughter's face.

"Onkel Zeb and I will komm see it when you're done, ain't so, Onkel Zeb?"

"For sure," Zeb said. "Don't forget to water the seeds when you get them in."

"We won't." Timothy grabbed Jessie's hand. "Let's hurry. I want to water." They started toward the door.

"I do, too." Becky, distracted, hurried after them.

Zeb waited until they'd disappeared before he chuckled. "What one does, the other wants to do, as well. You boys were just the same when you were that age."

"I guess we were." For a moment his thoughts strayed to Aaron, his youngest brother. What was he doing out there in the Englisch world? Was he well? Did he ever regret jumping the fence?

But there was little point in worrying over something he couldn't control or asking questions with no answers. He had enough of that right here at home.

Somewhat to his surprise, Caleb found he had little trouble figuring out how to work from the chair. He and Zeb labored together as they always did, with the exception that Zeb fetched things he couldn't reach. His spirits began to lift. Maybe he wasn't so helpless after all.

Zeb hammered a nail into place. "Folks were sure glad to see you at worship yesterday. Seemed like it had been an awful long time."

"For me, too." He frowned slightly. "Jessie was quiet after we got back from church, ain't so?"

His uncle considered, lean face solemn. "Maybe folks weren't as happy to wilkom her as they were to see you."

"She doesn't know anybody, I guess, other than Leah and Sam and their family."

Zeb looked at him as if waiting for more. When it didn't come, he set a screw for the door with a tad more forced than necessary. "Whenever someone brings a visiting relative to worship, folks gather round to meet them. Make them feel at home."

"So?" Maybe he knew where Zeb was going with this, but he didn't want to admit it.

"So, did you see anybody gathering around Jessie yesterday? I sure didn't. A few of the women smiled in passing, but that was about it."

"You think it's because they know she's Alice's cousin." He toyed with the nails in his hand, turning them over and over.

"Not just because she's Alice's cousin. Because most folks know how you feel about Alice and all of her kin."

Caleb tossed the nails into the toolbox. "I never said a word to anyone."

"You didn't have to. You think folks are dummies? They know you well, Caleb. Your actions speak louder than your words. Half the county probably knows you feel like Jessie pushed her way in here."

Caleb wanted to defend himself. Unfortunately, the small voice of his conscience was telling him there was something in what his uncle said.

If Jessie meant what she said to him earlier about making up for what Alice had done... But he didn't know for sure. Maybe she was trying to justify her own actions.

Or was he just trying to justify his?

Chapter Seven

Jessie sat in the rocking chair that evening, working her way toward the bottom of the mending basket. The room had a pleasant feeling of peace with the day's work done. Onkel Zeb was replacing the wheels on a broken toy while Becky and Timothy built a barn with blocks.

She shot a quick glance at Caleb. Once again he was holding a newspaper, but he didn't seem to be reading it. Did her very presence make him uneasy in his own home?

Jessie pushed that idea away. She had to be patient, and so did Caleb. Today she had referred to Alice very obliquely, and he hadn't bitten her head off. Maybe that was progress.

"We need some more pieces for the roof," Becky said. "Where are the rest of the green ones?"

"I'll find them." Timothy's method of searching involved diving into the block box headfirst, giving them a view of the seat of his pants.

Jessie couldn't help smiling. Caleb, meeting her gaze, was smiling, as well, and for a moment they shared their amusement. Then Timothy resurfaced, red in the face, clutching the long green blocks they were using for the roof. "I got them."

He was taking the blocks to his sister when he noticed the small shirt Jessie had pulled out of the basket. He hurried over to her. "Hey, that's my shirt. It was lost."

"Not lost. Just hiding in the mending basket." She held it up against him and chuckled. "I think you won't be wearing this one again."

Timothy held his arm out to see how short the sleeve was. "I grew, didn't I?"

"That's certain sure. You're getting bigger all the time." Jessie folded the shirt on her lap. "What shall we do with it? Can I use it to make patches in a quilt?"

"Whose quilt? Will it go on my bed?"

"If you want." She might not possess the artist's eye for a quilt that her sister-in-law did, but she usually had something in progress, and she took a lot of satisfaction from the quilts she made.

"Can I help?" Becky still sat on the rug by the barn, but she was watching them.

"Yah, you can. Do you like to sew?"

"I never tried." She looked at her hands as if assessing the possibility of their wielding a needle.

"Well, then, it's time you did. We'll collect some quilt patches and plan a project for you."

Jessie was ridiculously elated. It was the first time Becky had shown any enthusiasm for doing something with her, and at six, it was time she was introduced to sewing. Normally a mother, grandmother or aunt would have done it already, but Becky was missing all of those.

And whatever memories she had of her mother must have been sad ones. She was five when Alice died—old enough to see, if not understand, those last weeks of life. If only Jessie had been able to convince Alice to stay with her instead of coming home...

But Alice was determined. She had left Caleb and the kinder when Timothy was just a baby, and she hadn't contacted anyone. The only explanation she'd left behind had been a short note saying she was sorry. Jessie had wondered about postpartum depression, but Alice had been dissatisfied with her life for a time before that pregnancy.

Jessie's family had searched, of course, but it was easy for an Amish person to hide in the Englisch world. It was only when Alice was seriously ill with the cancer that took her life that she'd resurfaced, announcing that she intended to go back to Caleb for whatever time she had left.

Jessie had tried to dissuade her. She'd written, urging Alice to reconsider, to live with her and let Jessie care for her. But Alice had thought she could reconcile with the family she'd left.

Jessie, convinced it could only cause harm, had taken an endless series of buses to get to the address in Chicago that Alice had given her, only to be too late. Alice had gone back to Caleb.

Jessie eyed him covertly. How had he taken Alice's return? He'd accepted her back into his house because she was his wife. But Jessie couldn't believe he'd been glad to see her. And under the circumstances...

It was past, and it was futile to go over it again, but Jessie longed to replace the unhappy memories Becky must have with some happier ones of Alice.

She was the only person who could tell the children stories of "when Mammi was a little girl," but Caleb wouldn't allow it.

Daniel came down the stairs just then, obviously dressed to go out. Zeb raised an eyebrow.

"Are you finally using the courting buggy for its right purpose, Daniel?"

Daniel gave a good-natured grin. "If that happens, I'll be sure to tell you. Tonight I'm meeting with that Englisch couple who's talking about having me do new kitchen cabinets for them." He shrugged. "Not sure it's the best thing for me right now, though."

"That would be a big job for you, ain't so?" Caleb looked concerned, and Jessie thought she knew why. He was afraid Daniel might turn the job down because he was needed to help Caleb. "Why wouldn't you take it?"

Daniel hesitated. "It'd take a lot of time. And an extra pair of hands, most likely. I'm used to working on my own."

"If you're thinking we need you here, don't." Caleb bit out the words. "I can hire another man if need be."

Daniel shrugged again. "We'll see what happens. I'd best find out what they want first." He scurried out as if eager to escape an argument.

Jessie bit her lip to keep from offering an opinion that wouldn't be welcomed. She realized the children were staring after their uncle, so she laid the mending aside.

"It's about time for bed. Shall we put away the blocks?"

For a moment she thought she'd have a protest on her hands, but after a quick look at her daadi's face,

Becky began cleaning up. Jessie helped Timothy slide the barn they'd built into a corner out of the way. As long as he didn't have to tear his barn apart, he seemed willing enough.

In a few minutes she was shepherding the kinder upstairs. At a guess, Zeb and Caleb would take advantage of being alone to discuss this possible job of Daniel's and how it would affect them.

When Becky and Timothy were ready for bed, they unfortunately didn't seem ready for sleep. That always seemed to be a problem as the days grew longer. The daylight slipping into the room around the window shades convinced little ones they should stay up longer, even when they could hardly hold their eyes open.

"Tell us a story, Cousin Jessie." Timothy paused in the act of jumping on his bed. "Tell us a story before we go to sleep."

Becky didn't seem to be listening. Or at least, she was pretending not to be interested, busy settling her Amish faceless doll under the covers.

"A story. Now, let me think." Jessie looked into Timothy's blue eyes, so like Alice's, and the idea popped into her head. She couldn't tell them about Alice—or could she? If she didn't use Alice's name, Caleb would never know. And she wouldn't really be breaking her agreement, would she?

After a short struggle with her conscience, she gave in to the temptation.

"Once upon a time there were two little Amish girls," she began. "Their names were…Anna and Barbie."

"Were they twins?" Becky's attention seemed to be caught.

"No, no, they weren't. Anna was the big sister, and Barbie was the little sister. But even though they weren't twins, they liked to do things together, and Barbie would always say, 'Me, too, me, too' whenever Anna was doing something."

"Like me," Timothy said, grinning.

"Like you," she agreed, reaching out to tickle him. "So one day, they decided to go up the hill and pick blackberries."

"It must have been summer," Becky said wisely.

"Yah, it was. August, when the wild blackberries are ripe. So they each took a pail, and they went up the path to where the blackberries grew." She noted that Timothy had stopped wiggling and settled onto his pillow.

"The berries were so big and fat and juicy that they couldn't stop. They'd picked half a pail full each in no time at all. Anna picked the ones up high, and Barbie picked the ones on the bottom. They were just talking about what to make with the berries when what do you think Barbie saw under the blackberry brambles?"

"A bird," Timothy murmured sleepily.

"No, a turtle," Becky said.

"You're both wrong. It was a great big black snake. When Barbie saw it, she let out a huge shriek, threw her bucket into the air and ran as fast as she could go down the path. And the snake, who had been taking a nice nap in the shade of the bushes, went spinning around in a big circle and raced up the hill in the opposite direction as fast as it could go."

Becky giggled. "The snake was scared, too."

"I wouldn't be scared…" Timothy's words were interrupted by a huge yawn.

Jessie tucked the covers around him. "So Anna picked up all the berries she could find and took them back down the hill. Anna and Barbie helped their mammi make a big blackberry cobbler for supper, and they each had two pieces."

His eyes were closed. Jessie bent and kissed his cheek lightly. Then she went to Becky's bed. To her pleasure, Becky let her tuck the covers in and didn't even turn her face away from Jessie's kiss.

"Good night. Sleep tight," Jessie murmured. She went softly across the room and out into the hall.

When she turned from closing the door, her pulse gave a little jump. Zeb stood a few feet away.

"Ach, you startled me," she said softly. "I didn't know you'd komm upstairs."

"Just wanted my pipe." He gestured with it and then glanced at the door to the children's room. "I was in time to hear the story you were telling the kinder."

Something about his steady regard made her nervous. "Picking blackberries. It was maybe not as exciting as Onkel Daniel's version of fairy tales."

"It's best not to be too exciting when they're going to sleep, ain't so?" He paused for a moment. "Thing is, I'd heard that story before."

Jessie's breath caught. "When…when was that?"

"A long time ago now. Alice happened to see a black snake in the garden. Scared her, I guess. She mentioned the day she went picking berries with her big cousin and saw the snake."

Jessie pressed her hands together. She'd never thought of that. "Does Caleb know?" If he did, and the kinder mentioned the story…

Zeb shook his head. "He wasn't here that day. She

didn't want him to know she'd been so foolish, she said."

"I see." She tried to still her whirling thoughts. "Are you going to tell Caleb I told the kinder a story about their mammi?"

Zeb lifted an eyebrow. "I didn't hear you mention Alice, ain't so?"

Jessie felt herself relax. "I don't wish to upset Caleb, but it seems…"

"Yah, I know." Zeb's voice sounded weary. "No good can come of bottling everything up. I've tried and tried to convince Caleb of that, but he isn't ready to listen."

"No." They stood together for a moment, and she knew that they understood each other. "I haven't repeated that story to anyone in a long time. But it…it made my little Alice seem real to me again. Maybe one day, the kinder will remember it and know it was about their mother."

"Maybe one day you'll be able to tell them yourself," Zeb said.

"Maybe," she echoed, but she doubted it.

"I like scrambled eggs better than anything." Timothy was his enthusiastic self at breakfast a few days later. "Don't you, Onkel Daniel?"

Daniel considered, head tilted and eyes twinkling. "Better than chocolate cake? Or whoopie pies?"

"Well, but…I mean for breakfast. Cousin Jessie wouldn't give us whoopie pies for breakfast."

Caleb glanced at his son. Funny how quickly Timothy had accepted Cousin Jessie as the authority on what he had for breakfast. After a week, he acted as if Jessie had been here forever.

At the moment, Jessie was entering into the fun, talking about how a whoopie pie could be a breakfast food and making Timothy giggle. She seemed to have overcome whatever had depressed her spirits on Sunday.

Maybe Zeb had been wrong in what he'd thought was going on. Maybe people were sensible enough to know that Jessie wasn't responsible for what Alice had done. The thought made him uncomfortable. Why was it sensible for others to think that when he himself acted as if blaming Jessie was okay?

He risked a glance at her face again. He didn't blame her, exactly. He just didn't like being constantly reminded of Alice. That was natural enough. Not Jessie's fault, but not his fault, either.

"More coffee?" Jessie had just filled Onkel Zeb's cup, and she stood next to Caleb, the coffeepot in her hand.

He nodded and watched the hot liquid stream into the heavy white cup he used. A simple gesture, refilling the coffee cups, but one that Alice had ignored often enough. It was a silly thing to have bothered him. After all, he could pour his own coffee.

"Maybe a little slice of that shoofly pie with my coffee," Daniel said. "A man's got to keep his strength up, after all." He grinned, looking as if he expected a tart response to that.

"You'll need it, if you're going to take on that kitchen job," Onkel Zeb said. "Did you make up your mind yet?"

Daniel shook his head as Jessie put a slab of

shoofly pie in front of him. "Still have to work out all the figures before we get to an agreement. And I may not have the time and manpower to do it."

"I told you I'd hire another person to help on the farm until I'm rid of this cast." Caleb knew he sounded testy, but he couldn't help it.

Daniel eyed him. "Not so easy as you might think. Thomas is a fine helper, but I'm not sure where we'd find another like him."

"We can manage," Zeb said. "If someone has two good legs, I can teach him what to do."

"Is it possible…" Jessie began, and then fell silent when they all looked at her.

"Go on, Jessie," Zeb urged. "You have an idea?"

"Well, I just wondered if maybe there were things Caleb could do to help Daniel with the project—things he could do from the wheelchair that would free up Daniel's time."

Caleb swallowed his instant response. He shouldn't reject the idea just because it came from Jessie.

Daniel brightened, but then shook his head when Caleb didn't respond. "It would be too much for him."

"No. It wouldn't." No matter where the idea came from, it was a logical one. "If you lowered one of the work benches so I could reach it from the chair, there's plenty I could do. Better than sitting here feeling useless."

"That could make all the difference." Daniel gulped down the rest of his coffee and pushed his chair back. "I'll get started on those figures. Maybe you can come out to the shop after your exercises and we'll see if we can make it work." He beamed at Jessie. "Gut thought, Jessie."

Becky's fork clattered onto the table. "I'm done." She slid off her chair and started from the room.

"Take your plate to the sink first, please," Jessie said before Becky could make her escape.

"I want to go outside." Becky's face set in the pout that Caleb was seeing too often.

"Do as Cousin Jessie says, Becky." The least he could do was back Jessie up when she was right. Becky shouldn't be allowed to develop rebellious habits.

Becky just stared at him for a moment. Then, without a word, she came back, picked up her plate and utensils, and carried them to the sink.

"Denke, Becky," Jessie said. Ignoring Becky's lack of response, she began to clear the table with quick, deft movements. "When I've finished, will you be ready to start your exercises?"

Caleb suspected she thought he'd argue, but he wouldn't. He'd do whatever was necessary to get back to his normal self, including accepting help from Jessie.

By the time Jessie had pushed him through his first few exercises, Caleb was beginning to wonder if he really was willing to do anything to regain his strength. Jessie was much more of a taskmaster than he'd expected.

He stopped, panting a little at the exertion of attempting to lift his leg multiple times. "That's enough of that one."

"Just three more. Komm, you can do three more."

Caleb's temper flared in spite of himself. "I ought to know how many I can do."

"And what do you think the physical therapist would say to that?" she chided. "Now, if you were Becky's age, I could offer you a whoopie pie for doing it all ten times."

His momentary annoyance fizzled. "Are you saying I'm acting like a six-year-old?"

"What do you think?" Her eyes twinkled. "I'll help. Just three more."

Steeling himself, he managed to push himself through three more leg lifts.

"Wonderful gut," Jessie said. "You see? You can do whatever you put your mind to."

She sounded as if she had a routine for encouraging rebellious patients. "This can't be the first time you've done this—helped someone komm back from an injury, I mean."

"You remember all those brothers of mine, don't you? If one wasn't damaging himself, another one was. Mamm was too soft on them to make them exercise. And when Daad busted his leg…ach, if you think you're pigheaded, you should have seen my daad."

Jessie hadn't often relaxed like this when she talked to him. It was nice to see the affection in her eyes when she spoke of family.

She'd had a full, rich life in Ohio with her kin and her business, and she'd left it behind out of her need to help his family. She'd come here knowing what her reception would most likely be. He thought of what Zeb had said about the attitude of the church family and felt a prickle of guilt.

"It's gut you had a chance to get acquainted with Leah so fast. She's been a wonderful gut neighbor to us."

"I can see that. It's been nice to get to know her a little and to feel she's ready to be friends. Especially since I don't know any other women here."

Caleb hesitated, but Zeb's words still rankled. "Did you talk to some of the other women after worship?"

"A few." Jessie's gaze slid away from his, and she busied herself getting out the elastic bands for his next set of exercises.

"Some of them must have made you feel wilkom." He was pushing, because he needed to know if his uncle had been right or not.

Jessie was silent for a long moment. At last she shrugged. "I'm sure they usually do so. But folks here know I'm Alice's cousin. They're bound to be resentful. I can't be surprised that they are not eager to accept me."

Caleb's fingers tightened on the arms of the chair. "You mean it's because of me. Because I am unforgiving." He stopped, aghast at what he'd said. To be lacking in forgiveness for the wrongs done to him by another person was to live in defiance of God's law.

"I don't... I didn't mean that," he said quickly, stumbling over the words. "I've forgiven Alice." *Over and over.* So why did he have to keep doing it?

"Have you?" Jessie's face twisted in what he thought was grief and hurt. "Sometimes I think forgiveness has to keep happening again and again, each time we think of the person who has wronged us. Until one day, we finally know we are free, and can think of them without pain."

He felt he was seeing Jessie for the first time. She might act sure of herself and competent, but inside there was pain and guilt.

"Yah." He found he was reaching out instinctively, clasping her hand in his. He could feel the flutter of her pulse against his skin and hear the catch in her breath. "Have you been able to forgive her and be free?"

Jessie's eyes met his, and the barriers between them slipped away for the moment, at least. She sighed. "I'm getting better at it, I think. Maybe, one day…"

"One day," he echoed. He would like to live without this tight ball of anger and resentment inside him. He just didn't know how to get rid of it.

Her lips trembled a bit. "If I can help Becky and Timothy, perhaps I will go the rest of the way."

The lump in his throat made it hard to get the words out, but they had to be said.

"I'm sorry. Sorry I've made it more difficult for you, sorry for treating you as if you were to blame." His fingers moved against her skin. "Forgive me."

Whatever she might have answered was lost in a cry from the doorway. He turned, still clasping Jessie's hand, to find his daughter standing there, staring at them.

"Daadi! What are you doing?"

The anger in her small face shocked him. Maybe Jessie was right. Maybe Becky did need help.

"I am thanking Cousin Jessie for assisting me with my exercises," he said evenly. Jessie slipped her hand from his and stepped away, bending to pick up the exercise bands. "And you are being rude, Rebecca. You had best go to your room and think on it."

Becky stared at him with angry eyes. Then, with a sharp, cutting look at Jessie, she turned and ran toward the stairs.

Chapter Eight

Jessie couldn't get the expression on Becky's face out of her mind. She had been angry, yah, but upset, too. And then there were her own emotions to contend with. Maybe Caleb hadn't felt anything. Maybe it had all been her—her longing, her imagination, creating a momentary link that hadn't been real.

Caleb had certainly been quick to get back to his exercises after the interruption. Everything they had said to each other was strictly business. The minute they'd finished, he had headed out to the workshop, waving away her offer of help.

Thankfully Daniel must have been watching for him. From the kitchen window she saw Daniel hurry from his shop along the gravel lane to intercept his brother and push the wheelchair on its way. The shop was even farther from the house than the barn. Caleb was stubborn, that was all. She just hoped he wasn't so stubborn he'd hurt himself.

Jessie turned away, occupying herself with the fabric fragments she'd been gathering for the quilt project she wanted to start with Becky. A small nine-patch quilt, suitable for a doll's cradle—that was a good beginner project. In fact, it was the one her mamm had started her on all those years ago.

Mamm would have done the same with Alice. Jessie felt sure of it, even though she didn't remember the specifics. Mamm had been determined to do all she could after Alice's mother passed.

Jessie had enough scraps to start the doll quilt. Whether she'd have any cooperation from Becky was another question.

Picking up her sewing bag, she went into the hall and called up the stairs. "Becky and Timothy? Komm down for a minute, please."

Timothy bounded down the steps as he always did, his feet thudding on each tread. Becky came more slowly, running her hand along the rail. Jessie had thought she might have been crying but could see no sign of tears on her face.

"I have my sewing bag here, and I thought maybe you'd like to start on a sewing project. There are a lot of scraps in the scrap bag, so we could make a little quilt or maybe a pot holder together."

Timothy would no doubt want to do whatever his sister did, but the project she had in mind for Becky would be beyond his abilities. Still, she could find something to keep him busy.

"I want to make something." Timothy ran over to her and tugged on the bag. "Komm on, Becky."

"No." When they both looked at her, Becky managed to ignore Jessie. "I'm going to collect the eggs. Komm with me, and I'll show you how to do it."

Timothy looked a little hesitant, and Jessie suspected she knew why. He was a bit scared of the chickens, especially the bad-tempered Rhode Island Red.

"You're not scared, are you?" Becky knew just how to prompt him to do what she wanted.

"I'm not scared of any chicken. I'll get the basket." He ran toward the back door, and Becky followed him.

Jessie set her sewing bag on the floor next to the rocker. She'd known this wouldn't be easy, especially with Becky. Maybe she should have waited a bit longer to allow time for her to get over her little snit at seeing her daadi holding Jessie's hand.

At the moment, she'd best get outside so she could keep an eye on the egg gathering from a distance. She could logically be checking on the garden, couldn't she?

Jessie was bending over a few green leaflets that were already above ground while she watched the children approach the chicken coop. Becky, carrying the egg basket, unhooked the door and stepped right in. Timothy held back for a minute as the hens rushed toward Becky in hope of food. Then Becky said something to him, and he stepped into the enclosure.

If this helped Timothy get over his fear, it would be a good thing. He followed his sister under the shelter of the roof where the laying boxes waited. If the hens had been cooperative, this shouldn't take long.

Jessie let her gaze stray toward the workshop. How was Caleb getting along? If only he could do something, even if it wasn't his usual work, he'd be happier. Time hung heavy when a busy person suddenly had no responsibilities.

A squawk from the henhouse captured her attention. She craned her neck, trying to make out what was happening. Timothy's voice alerted her—he was yelling for his sister, and the red hen was chasing him.

Jessie got up quickly. Before she could go more than a few steps, Becky had reached her brother. She shoved him out the door and slammed it behind her. Timothy let out an anguished howl, and Jessie ran. That wasn't fear. It was pain.

When Jessie reached them, both children were outside the chicken coop. Becky was crying nearly as hard as Timothy was.

Jessie caught them, turning them toward her. Her heart pounded so loudly she could hardly hear. "What's happened? Who is hurt?"

They both tried to answer at once, and she could make no sense of it at all.

"Hush, now. I can't understand you when you're crying. Who is hurt?"

Becky managed to check her sobs. "Timmy. I didn't mean it. I slammed the door on his finger."

"Ach, now, we know you didn't mean it." She drew Timothy close against her. "Komm, Timothy. You must let me see your finger so I can tell how badly it's hurt."

"Don't touch it," he cried. Reluctantly he held his hand out, and she took it gently in hers.

"I think maybe you'll live, ain't so?" The small finger was red and puffing up a little, and an open scrape didn't make it look any better. But judging by the way he was moving his finger, it probably wasn't broken. He started to cry again, and she picked him up, holding him close against her.

"It will be all right. I promise. Komm, Becky. Let's go in the house and fix your bruder's finger, okay?"

Tears still dripped down Becky's cheeks, but she nodded. At least they'd both stopped wailing. Jessie took a cautious look toward the workshop, but obviously the men hadn't heard the commotion. Just as well. She'd like to get everyone calmed down and cleaned up before trying to explain this to Caleb.

Becky hurried ahead of her to hold the door open, and they went into the kitchen. Still cradling Timothy against her shoulder, Jessie pulled a handful of ice from the gas refrigerator.

"Becky, will you get a clean dish towel from the drawer for me?"

Nodding, Becky hurried to obey. Having something useful to do seemed to calm her tears a little. She rushed back with the towel.

Jessie sat down at the table with Timothy on her lap, detaching him from her shoulder. "We're going to put ice on your finger. That will help it stop hurting. Will you let Becky hold your hand steady?"

Sniffling, Timothy nodded, extending his hand toward his sister. Suppressing a few sniffles of her own, Becky took his hand gingerly. She held it while Jessie wrapped the towel around the ice and put it gently against the injured finger. Timothy winced at first, but then he seemed to relax when he realized it wouldn't make matters worse.

"Gut job, Becky. Timothy is a brave boy, ain't so?"

"Is it broken? Like Daadi's leg?" Becky's voice wavered.

Timothy actually brightened at that idea, convincing Jessie that he wasn't badly hurt. "Will I get a cast?"

"No, I don't think it's broken. But it has a nasty

scrape. We'll need to put a bandage on it, won't we, Becky?"

Becky nodded and ran to the kitchen drawer where first aid supplies were kept. She brought the whole box back with her.

"Gut. We'll keep the ice on just a little longer, I think." She affixed the bandage in place and held the ice against it, then tried a smile for the two of them, who still looked woebegone. "We're going to have to teach that red hen who is boss, ain't so?"

Becky's face seemed to crumple again. "It wasn't the hen. It was me. It's all my fault!" She bolted from the room before Jessie could stop her.

Jessie bit her lip. She'd tried not to interfere, but this time she had to. Becky couldn't go on like this, flaring up about things and then running off. Somehow she had to get through to the child.

But first, Timothy must be taken care of. His bottom lip was trembling again, no doubt in reaction to his sister's tears. She was reminded of her mother, saying that there were times when every mammi needed an extra pair of hands. Maybe she wasn't Becky and Timothy's mammi, but right now she was all they had.

"Becky feels bad because you got hurt, ain't so?" She smoothed Timothy's hair back from his rounded forehead. "She loves you."

Timothy snuggled against her. "Do you think Daadi cried when he got hurt?"

She suppressed a smile. "I'm sure he felt like crying, even if he didn't. Lots of times grown-ups do."

That seemed to satisfy him. After another minute of snuggling, he started to wiggle. "Maybe a cookie would make my finger feel better."

Jessie dropped a kiss on his hair. "I don't know about your finger, but I'll bet your tummy would like it. How about a snickerdoodle and a glass of milk?"

He nodded, and she set him on his own chair and got out the promised snack. He was using his hurt finger normally by the time he'd had a bite, so it was safe to assume he'd be okay. Now for Becky.

"I'll see if Becky wants a snack. You wait here for us, okay?"

"Okay," he said thickly around a mouthful of cookie.

With a silent prayer for guidance, Jessie climbed the stairs toward the children's bedroom.

Becky lay on her bed, both arms wrapped around her pillow. Her face was buried, but her shoulders still shook with muffled sobs. She looked so small and vulnerable that Jessie's heart ached.

She sat on the edge of the bed. When Becky didn't move, Jessie leaned over to put her hand on the child's back.

"Timothy is eating snickerdoodles. I think that means his finger feels much better. That's gut, ain't so?"

Becky didn't respond. Well, Jessie hadn't expected it to be as simple as that. Whatever troubled Becky, it was bigger than the question of her brother's finger.

"You feel bad because Timothy got hurt, I know. But it was an accident. Accidents happen to everyone. All we can do is try to be more careful."

That got a response from Becky. She shoved herself up on her elbows and pounded the pillow. "It's my fault! He's my little bruder. I have to take care of him."

"I know. I have little brothers, too." *And once I had*

a little cousin. "But we can't always stop them from getting hurt, no matter what we do."

"It's my fault. It's always my fault…just like when Mammi went away."

Jessie's heart seemed to stop. She had to repeat the words over in her own mind before she could take them in. Becky was blaming herself for Alice leaving. Why hadn't any of them seen that?

"Becky, listen…" She swallowed her words. Careful…she had to be very careful in what she said now. "Why would you think it was your fault that your mammi left?"

"Because it was. If I'd been better, or prettier, or…"

"Ach, Becky, don't!" She put her arm around the thin shoulders, ignoring the way Becky stiffened at her touch. "That's not true. It isn't. I know."

"How do you know? You weren't here." Becky's jaw set, reminding her of Caleb.

"No, I wasn't." *I wish I had been.* "But your mammi wrote to me all the time. Every week she wrote. And you know what she said about you?"

That caught Becky's attention. She actually turned to look at Jessie. "What?"

Jessie risked stroking her hair. "She said she had the prettiest little daughter ever. She told me all about what you did…when you took your first step, when you got your first tooth, everything. She was so very pleased with you, and she loved you so much."

"Then why did she go away?" The rebellious note was gone from her voice. Poor child. She wanted so much to know it wasn't because of her.

But how did Jessie answer her in a way that a six-year-old could understand? "I don't think even your mamm really understood why," she said carefully. "She was very young when she got married, and maybe she hadn't grown up enough yet. And sometimes she got really sad. Not because of what anyone did but just because of something inside her. It was like being sick. We don't blame people or get angry with them for being sick, do we?"

Jessie's own thoughts seemed to clarify as she tried to explain to the child. Who could say why Alice had been the person she was? Maybe having her mamm die when she was so young had started something inside her that none of them had understood.

"No, but…"

"No buts," Jessie said gently. "One thing we know for sure. It wasn't your fault that your mamm left. I promise."

Some of the tension eased out of Becky's face. She sat up, leaning against Jessie's arm for a precious moment before pulling away.

Becky wasn't entirely convinced. No one ever gave up a deeply held belief because of a few simple words.

Jessie knew that. She knew because looking into Becky's face was like looking into a mirror and seeing her own pain.

Just like Becky, she'd been telling herself that what Alice did was her fault. But Alice, no matter what problems she had, had been a grown woman, not a little girl.

There might be nothing Jessie could do about her own feelings, but there was something she had to do about Becky's. She must talk to Caleb about this, whether he wanted to hear it or not. Healing Becky's hurt would take effort on all their parts, not just on hers.

* * *

Caleb pushed the wheelchair through the back door and into the kitchen. No help needed, he told himself. There might be things he couldn't do, but he wasn't helpless, and that was a wonderful gut feeling.

He found Jessie alone in the kitchen, cutting up a chicken at the counter. "Chicken tonight, yah?"

He'd keep the talk between them light and casual. No more conversation that led to revealing emotions, and definitely no more touching. He still seemed to feel her pulse beating against his palm, and that wouldn't do.

Jessie's smile seemed a little strained. She was probably as uncomfortable about what had passed between them as he was. Not that it had meant anything.

"Chicken and homemade noodles, just like my grossmammi always made."

"I remember." Jessie's family had spread the wilkom mat on his first visit to Ohio, and her mother and grandmother had stuffed him until he was ready to burst. "Are yours as gut as hers?"

"I wouldn't go that far," she said lightly. She glanced at the clock. "You were out at the shop for two hours or more. You must be ready for a rest."

He shook his head, helping himself to a snickerdoodle from the cookie jar. "It felt great to be working again. Not that I'm anywhere near the craftsman Daniel is. He always had a feel for wood, even when he was a kid. I'm an apprentice compared to him."

"Even an apprentice can be helpful," she said, moving the heavy Dutch oven onto the stove. "This job… it's important to Daniel, ain't so?"

"Very. If he satisfies an Englisch client, he'll probably get a lot more orders. He shouldn't miss a chance like that. Even if all I can do is attach hinges and finish the wood, it frees Daniel up to do the hard part."

Jessie leaned against the sink, drying her hands. "You could reach everything all right?"

"Daniel fitted up a makeshift workbench that's just the right height for me." He slapped his palms on the arms of the chair. "Even if I'm stuck in this thing, I can still work. I…"

Caleb stopped. Here he was blabbing away about it as if he was some kind of hero for helping his brother, after all Daniel was doing for him. That was bad enough, but worse, he'd completely ignored the fact that it had been Jessie's suggestion in the first place.

Jessie was looking at him with some concern, probably because he'd stopped what he was saying in midstream. He shook his head.

"Ach, I'm forgetting the most important thing. You're the one who thought of it to begin with. Denke, Jessie."

She gave a quick shrug. "You would have, I'm sure."

Maybe, but she had first. He glanced around the kitchen, belatedly aware of how quiet it was. "Where is everyone?"

"Your uncle had to run over to the feed mill, so he took Becky and Timothy with him. They should be back soon." Now it was her turn to hesitate. "While they're out, I'd like to have a word with you about Becky."

"If it's about her being sassy this morning…" He was caught in a cleft stick. He could hardly say it was none of her business when she was taking care of his kinder.

"No, not that." A faint flush rose in her cheeks. "It's something that happened later. She told Timothy she'd show him how to gather the eggs from the chickens, so they went out to the coop."

If that was all, it hardly seemed worth her bringing it up. "I'm surprised he went. He's a little bit scared of the chickens."

"I know. But he wanted to appear brave to his sister, so he went." She hesitated. "I know Becky does that by herself, but I kept an eye on them since Timothy was going."

Caleb gave an impatient nod. Jessie was picking her words carefully over nothing, it seemed.

"I heard a ruckus and went running. I'm not sure exactly what happened, but I think that bad-tempered red took off after him. He was trying to get out, and in all the fuss, Becky accidentally shut the door on his finger."

"He's all right?" He must have been, if he'd gone off to the feed mill with Onkel Zeb.

"He's fine." Her face relaxed in a smile. "I think they were both more scared than anything. I took care of the scraped finger, and Timothy was happy again in no time."

"Well, then…"

"But Becky wasn't." Jessie looked at him, her hazel eyes dark and serious. "I found her upstairs crying her heart out. She was blaming herself, you see, for Timothy getting hurt."

He frowned. "I'm more used to boys than girls. I

don't recall my brothers being upset about something like that, but Becky is more sensitive. That's all."

"You're thinking I'm making a mountain out of a molehill."

Jessie's comment was so near the truth that he had to smile. "Aren't you?"

"It was what else she said that troubles me." Jessie took a breath. "She said she was to blame for Timothy getting hurt. Just as she was to blame for her mammi going away."

The words hit Caleb like a blow to the stomach. For an instant it seemed the wind had been knocked out of him. He finally got his breath so he could speak. "She couldn't think that."

"She does." Jessie's lips trembled. "I'm sorry. I know you don't want to hear it. And you don't want me to mention Alice. But it's no use trying to handle her leaving and her dying that way. Don't you see?" She leaned toward him, almost pleading. "Becky has that guilt in her heart, foolish as it is. You can't make it go away by pretending it isn't there."

He spun the chair away from her, because he was afraid of what his own face might betray. "Didn't you tell Becky she was wrong?"

"Of course I did." Now it was Jessie who sounded impatient. "I tried to get through to her. I told her how often her mammi talked about her in letters, and how happy she was to have a sweet little daughter." Jessie's voice tightened on that. "Alice did love them, you know. Despite what she did."

Caleb wanted to push everything away, because it hurt too much to talk about it. But Jessie... Jessie had come too far into their lives for that, like it or not.

"I'll talk to her," he said, trying to sound sure of himself. "I'll convince her it wasn't her fault."

"I know you'll try to make it better. But it's not easy to let go of the burden of guilt, no matter how irrational it may be. Becky…"

"All right!" He couldn't take any more. "I'll do what I can. Just leave it alone for now."

Chapter Nine

Had Caleb tried to talk to Becky about her mother or not? Jessie sat with her sewing basket at her feet that evening, wondering. Somehow she thought not. Caleb's stoic expression might not reveal his emotions, but Becky would be showing the effects if he'd said anything.

Becky was quiet, for sure, but it was the same quiet that she'd maintained since her bout of crying earlier in the day. Maybe Caleb had had no opportunity to get Becky alone for a serious talk. Or maybe he was avoiding the job, unwilling to open that box of trouble.

Jessie could understand. It was always tempting to pretend that nothing was wrong, sometimes even convincing yourself. After all, she'd convinced herself that she'd done everything she could to keep Alice from coming back here to die. But had she? Had she been able to disentangle her own feelings from what was best for everyone?

And then there was the realization that she and Becky were doing the same thing—blaming themselves for what Alice had done. Becky was clearly wrong. She could have done nothing. Jessie would like to say the same of herself, but she couldn't quite convince herself.

Life could be like the tangle of thread she'd discovered in her sewing basket—impossible even to find an end to pull.

She could fix the thread with a pair of scissors. The same wasn't true of relationships among people.

Smoothing out a couple of the fabric squares she'd cut, she started to pin them together for a small quilt. Timothy, deserting his toy barn, came over to see.

"What are you making, Cousin Jessie?" He fingered one of the pieces and narrowly missed pricking himself on a pin. "What will it be?"

"It'll be a quilt when it's finished." She smiled at him. "But it won't have any pins in it then to stick you."

"Gut." He gave a little shiver as if imagining himself wrapped in a quilt with pins. "Can I do it?"

She glanced at Caleb, wondering if he'd object to his son learning to use a needle. But he seemed intent on something he was jotting on a tablet.

"Sure thing. Let me get you some pieces of your own to sew." She found a couple of scraps and held them together. "The needle goes down through the material and then back up through. Try putting it in right here."

His little face intent, tongue sticking slightly out of the corner of his mouth, he managed to push the needle through and promptly dropped it so that it hung by the thread. "I did it."

"Yah, you did. Now keep pulling on the needle until the thread is tight. Next we'll come back up through the material." Experience with her small nieces and nephews had taught her that it was too much to expect him to make a complete stitch in one movement.

She took a covert look at Becky and discovered that she was watching them. Good. She was interested. Now to reel her in. "There's some material here if you'd like to try, Becky."

Becky hesitated and then came over. She stood in front of Jessie with her hands linked as if to show that she wasn't really all that intrigued.

"Why don't you pick out two pieces of different colors you think would look nice next to each other."

She handed Becky the basket and began threading a needle for her, stopping only to help Timothy in his efforts to stab the material without stabbing himself.

In a moment Becky had pulled a stool over and settled in next to Jessie. As she'd imagined, Becky's little fingers were quite nimble, and she soon got on to the idea of making small, even stitches. Her line of stitches wasn't quite straight, but it was very good for a first try.

"Look at that. You've done this before, haven't you?"

Becky smiled. "Leah showed me a little bit, and I practiced. It's fun."

"My fingers are tired," Timothy announced. "I need to put my horse in the barn." He dropped his material in Jessie's lap and reached for the horse, then paused. "Tell us another story about the big sister and little sister. Is there one with a pony in it?"

Jessie really didn't want to tell her thinly disguised story in front of Caleb, but it seemed her chickens had come home to roost. She glanced at Zeb, who gave a tiny shrug. At least Caleb wasn't paying much attention.

"Once upon a time, Anna was teaching Barbie how to drive the pony cart. Their pony was named Snowflake. Know why?"

Timothy blinked, shaking his head, but Becky grinned. "It was white, ain't so?"

"That's right. It was a pretty little white pony, but when they drove the cart through a puddle, she got all muddy. So they decided to give her a bath."

She spun out the story, seeing that Timothy's eyes were growing heavy while he listened. He leaned against her knee, patting the toy horse.

"So when the pony was sparkling clean, Anna and Barbie led her up toward the house to show Mammi. But they didn't watch where they were going, and before you knew it, Snowflake saw a nice freshly plowed garden and thought it would be a great place to roll."

Timothy started to giggle, anticipating what the pony would do, and Becky grinned.

"So Anna and Barbie grabbed the rope and pulled as hard as they could, but they couldn't stop that determined pony. She rolled and rolled right in the dirt. And then she stood up and shook herself, and the wet dirt flew all over Anna and Barbie until they were even dirtier than Snowflake. Mammi came out, and they thought she'd be mad, but instead she laughed until the tears rolled down her cheeks."

The kinder laughed almost as much as Mammi had that day, especially Timothy, who found the image of the mud-splattered little girls hilarious.

Once again, just telling the story seemed to bring Alice alive again for her. It hurt, yes, but at the same time it was comforting. Those we lost did live on in our memories, it seemed.

"Time to get ready for bed," she said firmly when Timothy suggested another story. She shooed them toward the stairs and was about to follow when Caleb said her name.

Jessie paused, looking back at him.

"That story…" Caleb hesitated. "Would I be right in thinking it a true story?"

So he knew. Had Alice told him at some point, or was it just obvious from her own emotions?

"Yah, it was true."

He nodded, his eyes going dark with pain. "I thought so."

She waited for him to forbid it, but the words she anticipated didn't come.

"All right," he said at last. "All right." His voice was heavy, and her heart ached for him. But she knew better than to comfort him. He couldn't accept that, not from her.

Caleb stared down at the cast on his leg for a few minutes, hearing the sound of Jessie's retreating footsteps. He'd been so sure he was right to forbid any talk about Alice. That part of their lives was over, and the best thing they could do was forget.

But he'd been wrong, if doing so had allowed his daughter to blame herself. He still wasn't sure how to fix it, but perhaps letting Jessie tell her stories was a step in the right direction.

"Something is wrong," Onkel Zeb observed. "Will you tell me?"

Caleb moved his shoulders restlessly, trying to

get rid of the weight of the guilt. "I'm not hiding it," he muttered, knowing that was exactly what he was doing. From himself, most of all. "Becky got upset this morning, and she told Jessie something she's kept secret from the rest of us." He forced himself to display a calm he didn't feel. "Becky says it's her fault that her mother went away."

For a long moment there was silence. Onkel Zeb shook his head slowly, his face sorrowful. "Poor child. Poor little child."

"I should have known." The truth burst out on a wave of pain. "I should have been the one to find out, not Jessie."

"Maybe it was easier for Becky to say it to Jessie instead of you."

"I'm her daad. She barely knows Jessie." Resentment edged his tone.

"How could Becky tell you?" He asked the question and just let it lie there between them. Onkel Zeb had always done that when the brothers tried to evade responsibility that belonged to them. His uncle looked at him steadily until Caleb's gaze fell.

Caleb's throat grew tight. "I never spoke of her mother. She must have thought she couldn't. So she kept it to herself. Brooded on it, most likely. And I never realized."

That was the bitterest thing of all—he hadn't realized something was wrong. Becky had lost all the laughter and sunshine she'd once possessed, and he hadn't even guessed at the cause.

"It won't be easy to change her mind," Zeb observed.

"That's what Jessie said. It will take more than

just telling her it's not her fault to make her really believe it."

"Cousin Jessie has a gut heart," his uncle observed. "And a sharp eye where the kinder are concerned."

"I don't deny that. I just wish…"

He didn't know what he wished. That she'd never come here? But if he hadn't broken his leg, if she hadn't come and insisted on staying in spite of his order, how long would it have taken him to find out what was happening with his daughter?

"Your parents' failings hurt all three of you boys." His uncle's voice was heavy. "Look at the results. You married a girl who was nowhere near ready to be a wife and mother. Daniel smiles and guards his heart from love. And Aaron runs away entirely."

"You can't blame all that on Mamm and Daad. They didn't mean to hurt us."

"Not meaning to has caused a lot of trouble." Onkel Zeb sounded more severe than Caleb could ever remember. "And now you. You didn't mean to hurt Becky by your silence. But it happened. If you are not careful, your kinder will be as afraid of loving as you are."

Caleb wanted to argue. The words boiled inside him, but he couldn't let them out. If there was even a chance that Onkel Zeb was right, he must do something. Must change. And the pitiful thing was that he didn't know how.

"Onkel Daniel says he saw a few ripe strawberries in the strawberry patch." Jessie kept a firm hold on Timothy's hand as they approached the patch that lay between the barn and Daniel's workshop. He was only too likely to run right over the plants in his eagerness.

"I want to pick lots," he exclaimed.

"It's too early for there to be lots," Becky said wisely.

"That's right." Jessie smiled at her, relieved that Becky seemed a little more herself this morning.

"Not like when Anna and Barbie picked the blackberries," Becky said, eyes already focused on the green plants. "Maybe we can have enough to eat, though."

"Or make a rhubarb strawberry cobbler. Onkel Zeb said Daadi loves that," Jessie said. Jessie stopped at the edge of the strawberry patch and knelt to capture Timothy's wandering attention. "We walk only on the path between the plants, ain't so? And we move the leaves very, very gently to look."

"And only pick the really red ones," Becky added. "I'll watch him, Cousin Jessie."

Jessie nodded. Becky still wanted to look out for her little brother, and that was how it should be. But she didn't seem quite so determined to push Jessie out of the picture.

Could Jessie say the same for Caleb? Maybe, at least a little. He could have been angry the previous night when he'd realized her stories were about Alice. He hadn't been. Grieved, yes, but he would put his own pain aside if it meant helping his children.

"I found some," Timothy shouted, and Jessie stepped carefully over the row to look.

"Yah, those are fine to pick. Yum, they'll be delicious."

"I got some, too," Becky began, and then gave a startled yelp. "Look what's here! Komm, schnell."

Jessie picked Timothy up and swung him over the

row of plants he was about to step on. They found Becky squatting next to a turtle.

"Not a snake, like the story. A turtle," Becky said. She touched the shell with the tip of her finger. "Is it dead?"

"No, he's just hiding in his shell. He's afraid of boys and girls, I think. He's called a box turtle."

"Why?" Timothy wanted to know.

Jessie grinned. "I have no idea. But my daadi said that's what this kind of turtle was, and I believed him."

"Did you find one when you were my age?" Becky asked.

"Just about. My brother and I were picking strawberries when we found him. We put our initials on his shell, so whenever we saw him we knew he was our friend."

"Can we do that?" Becky jumped up. "I'll get a crayon."

"We need something more lasting than crayon. Why don't you run over to the shop and ask Onkel Daniel for a permanent marker?"

"Okay." Becky leaped over the rows of berry plants and streaked off toward the shop.

"Does the turtle eat the berries?" Timothy clutched his berry container close to his chest.

"I don't know, but I'm sure there will be enough for all of us. You could watch him and see."

Timothy squatted, staring intently at the turtle, who seemed equally intent on staying safe in his shell and peering out at Timothy.

Amused, Jessie concentrated on picking the ripe berries along the edges of the rows. If the children's attention lasted, they might get a pint or more, and the berries along the edges should be picked before they attracted the attention of hungry birds.

"Daadi's coming," Timothy said, looking up from his absorption.

Jessie's heart gave a little thump when she spotted Becky pushing the wheelchair toward them while Caleb propelled the wheels with his hands. She almost jumped up to help but caught herself. Better to let Becky do it and give them a chance to talk.

But it looked as if their thoughts were only on the turtle. Becky waved a marker in one hand. "Daadi wants to see, too."

"We'll bring the turtle to him." Jessie picked the creature up carefully and carried it to a spot on the edge of the patch where Caleb could examine it easily.

"Here we are. I suspect he'll stay in his shell until we leave. Becky, will you put a *B* for Becky or an *R* for Rebecca?"

Becky knelt, uncapping the marker. "A *B*, 'cause mostly I'm Becky. Where shall I put it, Daadi?"

Caleb gave the question serious consideration, but his eyes twinkled a little. "Why don't you do one side and let Timothy do the other?"

Becky nodded and advanced the marker toward the shell. She hesitated, the pen wavering a bit. "Cousin Jessie, will you hold it still?"

It seemed highly unlikely the turtle would venture out of its shell, but she nodded, steadying it until Becky had put a small *B* on one side.

"Now me, now me!" Timothy squished his way between them. "Hold him still, Cousin Jessie."

"Gently now," Jessie cautioned.

"You don't need to press hard," Caleb added, lips quirking as he and Jessie exchanged a glance.

Jessie's heart warmed for no good reason. But just for a moment he'd reminded her of the optimistic young man she'd spent an afternoon with a long time ago.

And lost my heart to, a small voice whispered. She did her best to ignore it.

"Sehr gut," she said when Timothy had managed a wobbly *T* on the ridged shell.

"Just like you did, ain't so?" he said, and turned to his father. "Cousin Jessie and her brother did that when they were our age."

"Did you ever put your initial on a turtle, Daadi?" Becky asked.

"No, I don't think so." Caleb hesitated, and Jessie saw his brown eyes darken a little. Odd how quickly she had learned to read his moods. He was thinking of something that saddened him.

Caleb reached out to pull Becky into the circle of his arm. "But once I put a *C* for Caleb and an *A* for Alice on that big old apple tree by the paddock. That was when I was courting your mammi." He smoothed a strand of Becky's hair back. "I'll bet you can find it if you look. Komm back and tell me, yah?"

Becky's eyes had widened at the mention of her mother. She nodded tentatively as if not sure that was the best thing to do. Then she ran off toward the apple tree, with Timothy in hot pursuit.

It took Jessie a moment or two to be sure she had mastery of her voice. "That was gut for her to hear, I think."

"I hope so." His voice was sober. "Onkel Zeb said…"

He let that trail off, and his face closed down. Apparently she wasn't meant to know what Zeb had said. But whatever it was, she suspected it was good advice. She was almost afraid to speak for fear of ruining the step forward he'd taken.

Caleb was looking after his children, who were circling the apple tree. "I hope you…we are right about this."

Her heart clutched at the way he'd coupled them together in the responsibility. "Yah."

Finally Caleb looked at her, something a little rueful in his gaze. "Any thoughts on what to do next?"

Was he seriously asking for her advice? She couldn't quite accept that he was relying on her, but she did have an answer if he wanted one.

"Becky said once that she didn't want to look like her mammi, because you wouldn't like that." She stopped, afraid she'd gone too far.

Caleb brushed a hand at his forehead as if brushing away cobwebs. "She does look like Alice. I never realized…" He shook his head slightly. "Becky shouldn't feel that way about how she looks. But being pretty isn't everything."

Jessie forced a smile. "I'm afraid it's the first thing a young man notices."

But he didn't put it off lightly. "A gut heart is worth more than a pretty face."

Did he mean that as a compliment? She found herself ridiculously elated, even while thinking that no woman especially wanted to be praised for her plain looks. Now, if a man found beauty in the person who had the good heart—well, perhaps that was reaching for the moon.

Jessie reminded herself that she had long since become satisfied with the life she had. It wouldn't do to let being here make her long for something that was out of reach and always had been.

Chapter Ten

It was an off Sunday, so Caleb wouldn't have to sit through another worship service wondering if folks were feeling sorry for him. Like most Amish church districts, worship here was held every other Sunday. In the intervening week, a family might travel to worship with a neighboring district or spend a peaceful day at family gatherings.

Peaceful. Somehow that didn't exactly describe today's visiting. The whole family was invited to Zeb's cousin Judith's house for her usual immense family meal, giving opportunities for everyone to speculate on Jessie's presence among them.

At the moment, he, Onkel Zeb and Daniel were lingering over coffee in the kitchen, watching Jessie packing the pies she'd made into a basket.

Daniel put his mug in the sink and went to peer over her shoulder. "You're not going to take all four pies to Cousin Judith's, are you? We'll be fortunate to get a slice. If you left them for us…"

"And go empty-handed?" She set the fourth pie on the rack in the basket. "We can't do that. And I don't think you'll go hungry if it's like any family meal I've ever gone to."

Daniel grimaced, and Caleb knew just what he was thinking. "The food will be wonderful gut, but I'd just as soon stay home if I had my way."

Before Jessie could react, Onkel Zeb chuckled. She looked at him inquiringly.

He grinned. "Ask Daniel why he doesn't want to see my cousin."

Jessie couldn't know it was a family joke, but she did as he directed. "Why, Daniel?"

"Onkel Zeb can laugh. It's not him she's after," Daniel grumbled. "Every single time I see Cousin Judith, she wants to know why I'm not married yet."

"And then she starts talking about all the young women she thinks would be perfect for him," Caleb added, grinning at his brother's discomfort. "If he's not quick on his feet, he'll find himself courting someone without even knowing it."

"You should talk," Daniel retorted. "She's starting to think about you now. She's probably lining up available widows. She says the kinder need—"

"Time to hitch up the carriage," Onkel Zeb said loudly, covering the end of that sentence.

For an instant Caleb was startled, but then he saw Becky and Timothy coming and understood. Just as well if the kinder didn't hear any speculation about him remarrying, which he wasn't going to do, anyway.

Jessie jumped into the momentary silence. "Becky, will you wrap up a couple of the oatmeal cookies for you and Timothy during the ride to Cousin Judith's?"

Becky's slight frown vanished, and she trotted over

to Jessie. "Two for Timothy and two for me, yah?" She reached for the cookie jar on the counter.

Caleb nodded. "That's gut. Timmy, you go along and help Onkel Daniel hitch up. It's time we were on the road."

The awkward moment passed. Daniel sent an apologetic glance toward Caleb and went out, Timothy at his heels.

He couldn't very well blame Daniel. Or Cousin Judith, for that matter. Speculation about the marital prospects of bachelors was common in the Amish community, and the blabbermauls had been gossiping about the King brothers for years.

Jessie was supervising while Becky tucked a snowy napkin over the pies in the basket. She seemed to have an instinctive awareness of Becky's need to help, and she went out of her way to invite that assistance. Jessie was thoughtful when it came to the children. He had to give her that. She seemed to have noticed things in a little over a week that he hadn't picked up on in a year.

He didn't like that idea, but he couldn't seem to dismiss it, either.

Soon they were all assembling outside to climb into the family carriage for the ride to the farm where Cousin Judith lived with her youngest son and his family. There were sure to be plenty of cousins and second cousins there, all curious about Jessie. Did Jessie realize that?

Her expression was as serene and composed as always, but he thought he detected a hint of worry in her eyes. While he wondered whether he should say something, Onkel Zeb supervised loading everyone into the carriage. Before Caleb quite understood what was happening, he found he was driving, with Jessie sitting beside him.

"You can tell Jessie about the valley along the way," Zeb said blandly. "She hasn't had a chance to see much of anything since she came."

What Jessie thought about that, Caleb couldn't say. She was glancing across the field, and the brim of her bonnet hid her face from him.

Daniel seemed to be teasing Becky in the back of the carriage—Caleb heard her giggle. He glanced back. "Don't get the kinder all riled up before we reach Cousin Judith's," he warned. "Not unless you want to be responsible for calming them down again."

"Hey, I'm just their onkel," Daniel protested. "I'm supposed to be fun."

"How about a game of I Spy?" Jessie suggested. "You can look for signs of spring. I spy a willow tree that has its leaves out. What do you see?"

Of course both of them started naming things, trying to top each other. Since Jessie couldn't very well keep turning around, Onkel Zeb and Daniel took over the game, and they were soon completely engrossed.

"That was a gut idea," Caleb said under the cover of their noise. "Denke, Jessie. Daniel always did like to stir things up."

"When he's a father, he'll learn," she said, smiling a little.

"If," Caleb muttered, thinking of what Zeb said about the influence their parents' troubles had on them.

She shrugged, obviously not wanting to venture an opinion on the subject.

They passed two other Amish buggies headed in the other direction, no doubt on the same mission they were. Each buggy had a husband and wife in the front, of course, and he was suddenly very conscious of Jessie sitting beside him. What was she thinking? Any casual observer might assume they were husband and wife.

Onkel Zeb had no doubt thought of that. He was getting as bound on mischief as Daniel was, in his own way. What did he think was going to happen?

Caleb had been silent too long, and he saw that Jessie was looking at him with apprehension. He cleared his throat, trying to find the right way to reassure her.

"I thought maybe…" He ran out of words, not sure what he wanted to say.

"Yah?" Her eyebrows lifted.

The game was still going full blast in the back of the carriage, and he and Jessie might as well have been alone. "If you're feeling a bit nervous about being pitchforked into a lot of family…well, I don't blame you, I guess."

"It is a little scary," she confessed. "I suppose I met some of them at…at the wedding." She rushed over that part. "But I probably won't remember names."

His jaw tightened at the mention of his wedding to Alice, but he forced himself to go on. "Nobody will expect you to, except probably Cousin Judith. You won't be able to dodge her."

"Wants to have a shot at me, does she?" Jessie seemed to make an attempt at lightness, but he didn't think she felt it.

"It's certain sure she'll want to know all about you and not be shy about asking." He should have realized it would be an ordeal for her, meeting all these people who had strong feelings about what Alice had done. "They'll be polite, I think." He hoped. "If you get caught in an uncomfortable conversation, you can always say you have to check on the kinder."

"I'll be fine." In a turnabout, she was the one reassuring him. "Denke, Caleb." She smiled, her eyes warming as she looked at him. "It's gut of you to think of it."

Her smile touched him. She was going into a difficult situation, but she wouldn't let it get her down. It seemed Jessie had a tough core of strength to go along with the tenderness she showed his kinder.

Looking back on it that evening, Jessie had to admit that the afternoon had gone better than she'd anticipated. Zeb's cousin Judith had been terrible inquisitive, that was certain, firing question after question at Jessie until she'd begun to sympathize with Daniel's reluctance to face her.

Then suddenly the inquisition stopped. Apparently she'd passed some sort of test and had gained Judith's grudging acceptance. And where Cousin Judith led, it seemed the rest of the family followed.

Jessie had come home with a copy of Cousin Judith's precious recipe for pon haus, she'd exchanged quilting ideas for youngsters with a second cousin who had daughters about Becky's age, and she felt she'd begun to make some friends.

Now the house was quiet. The kinder were long since asleep, and Daniel had gone off on some mission of his own that he'd seemed disinclined to talk about. A girl? She'd wondered but hadn't asked.

Onkel Zeb, suppressing his yawns, had headed for

bed early, and Caleb had disappeared into his own room at that point. Had he been reluctant to be left alone with her? She wondered, but her relationship with Caleb was tentative at best, so she tried to take things as they came.

Besides, she enjoyed these last few moments of tidying the kitchen for the next day, feeling the house sleep around her. It was almost as if she belonged here, as if this were her own house, her kinder asleep upstairs, her…

"Jessie, surely you can stop working now. It's late."

Startled, Jessie swung around from the sink to find Caleb in the doorway. The memory of the direction her thoughts had been headed made her cheeks warm.

"Ach, I'm enjoying it. My mamm always says that tidying the kitchen the last thing at night sets it up for a fine morning's start."

"Looks wonderful tidy to me already. You should see it when it's just us and Onkel Zeb here." He wheeled himself around the table, closer to her. "If it's Daniel's turn to do the dishes, they pile up until there aren't any left to eat from."

"He can't be as bad as all that. Although I confess, my brothers are a menace when left alone in the kitchen." She dried her hands on the towel. Was he hinting that it was time she retired to the daadi haus?

But he didn't seem in any hurry. "I remembered that I hadn't told you I have an appointment with the doctor tomorrow morning. The van is going to pick me up at nine."

"I should think he'll be happy with your progress. You're getting stronger every day." That wasn't an exaggeration. In the past week he'd done things he hadn't even attempted when she'd first come.

"Yah, it's been better. It's that boss I have forcing me to exercise, ain't so?"

When Caleb's eyes crinkled in amusement, his whole face changed, warming until she hardly remembered the steely expression he'd worn that first day. Her heart lifted in response, making her think she'd best give herself another lecture about her attitude toward Caleb.

"I'm only doing my job," she said, unable to keep from smiling back. "You're the one who is working hard at it. You have the will to get back to normal, and that's the most important part."

Getting back to normal. To Caleb, that meant seeing the last of her. Ironic that the harder she worked to help him, the sooner she'd leave.

"Being at Cousin Judith's today…it wasn't bad after all, ain't so?" he asked.

Her smile widened. "I began to sympathize with Daniel when she started questioning me. I felt like she turned my head inside out to see what was in there."

"Yah, Cousin Judith has that effect on people. She claims she's old enough to say what she wants, but as far back as I can remember, she always has. What was she asking you?"

Jessie hesitated, but he seemed to want to know. "Actually, she was asking about Alice. About why we were so close."

She waited for Caleb's expression to shutter as it usually did at the mention of Alice. But although he frowned, he didn't turn away from the subject.

"I guess she didn't know about Alice's mamm

dying when she was so young. I don't think we ever talked about it."

It was a measure of success that he acknowledged that much, she thought. "Yah, well, I don't suppose it mattered. She understood when she realized that Alice was much more like a little sister to me."

She darted a cautious glance at Caleb, and found that he was studying her gravely with a hint of question in his eyes.

"There's more to it than that," he said slowly, with an air of feeling his way. "It seems like you hold yourself responsible for…well, for what she did wrong."

Jessie brushed a hand across her forehead, trying to banish the memories. "Maybe so. I guess I never got over thinking that I had to take care of her."

He didn't speak for a moment, and the old farmhouse was very still around them…so still she could hear the ticking of the clock on the shelf.

"Why?" Caleb spoke abruptly. "Tell me why, Jessie." He reached out to circle her wrist with his fingers as if he'd compel her to tell him the truth.

She found she was shaking her head. "It…it's nothing."

Caleb leaned over to grasp one of the kitchen chairs and pull it close to the wheelchair. "Sit down and tell me. I want to know why it's important to you. You don't have to atone for what someone else did wrong."

Jessie sank down on the chair, as much because her knees were wobbly as because of the pressure of Caleb's hand. "I was the big sister. That's how my mamm put it after Alice's mother passed. She would try to be a mamm to Alice, and I must be her big sister."

Caleb nodded. "You mentioned that, and I could

just hear your mamm saying it." He waited as if he understood there was more she had to tell.

"I tried. I really wanted to be a gut big sister. But I failed." The taste of failure was still there. "I just… I suppose I got tired of always having to include her. One day, after school, we were walking home." The memory never really left her, but it wasn't easy to say out loud. "Alice got mad because I was talking with the other girls. I wasn't paying attention to her."

"Ach, Jessie, every big brother or big sister feels that way sometimes. Plenty of times I told Daniel and Aaron to get lost."

She couldn't smile as he'd obviously intended. "That's what she did. Really. She ran off into the woods and I…I didn't go after her. The other girls said she'd jump out at us when we got home, but she didn't. Alice was lost."

"What happened?"

"I went back. I looked in the woods, called to her, all the time getting more and more frantic. I couldn't find her. Finally I had to go home and tell Mamm and Daad what I'd done."

His fingers moved soothingly on the palm of her hand. "Somebody found her, yah? And she was all right?"

"Daadi called out all the neighbors. We searched and searched." She still remembered how terrifying it had been. "I followed along behind Daad, feeling so guilty. Someone finally found her asleep under a tree."

"So no harm was done." Caleb was obviously struggling to understand. "Maybe you were thoughtless, but that shouldn't make you carry a burden the rest of your life."

She shook her head. He didn't understand. Maybe he couldn't.

"I was responsible, but it was worse than that. When Alice flounced off into the woods, I was actually glad. I finally had time alone with my friends. Then, when I couldn't find her, I knew how wrong that had been."

"Ach, Jessie, if anybody could be too responsible, it must be you." His voice was gentle, maybe a little amused, but kind.

The trouble was that she couldn't tell him the rest of it, because it involved him too closely. How could she admit that she'd resented it when he picked Alice? How could she say that she might have kept Alice from coming back here to die if only she'd tried harder? Maybe she could have spared Caleb and the kinder if she'd been wiser and more determined.

"You want to make amends for the harm Alice might have done to Becky and Timothy." Caleb's fingers tightened on hers, and she forced herself to look at him. "I do understand that, Jessie. You came because you thought you could make a difference."

"Yah, I did." She was finding it difficult to breathe, sitting so close to him in the quiet house, feeling his hand encircling hers as if it was the most natural thing in the world. "You don't agree?" She made it a question, longing to have this much, at least, clear between them.

"At first all I wanted was to get rid of you, but…" His voice trailed off, and she felt his gaze on her face as if he were touching it. "You showed me some things about my kinder that I should have seen for myself, Jessie. I'm grateful." He leaned toward her, his eyes intent. "This hasn't been easy for you. I'm sorry if I made it harder."

She'd never expected an apology from him...never thought he'd admit that her presence had helped. She ought to have spoken, but her lips trembled.

Caleb was scanning her face. He was so close that she could see a miniscule scar on his temple, hear the intake of his breath.

"Jessie." He said her name softly. He leaned even closer...so close that in a moment their lips would touch.

And then footsteps sounded on the outside steps, and the back door rattled. Caleb snatched his hand away, spinning the chair around so that by the time Daniel came inside, they were several feet apart.

Jessie managed to compose herself, to speak rationally to Daniel. But all the while her heart ached. Now she'd never know if Caleb would have kissed her. And she'd never know if he was glad or sorry that Daniel had stopped him.

The next day, Caleb still couldn't quite believe his actions. How had he come so close to Jessie? Another moment and he'd have kissed her.

He could only be thankful Daniel had come in when he did. If Caleb had acted on the impulse of the moment, he'd have made all their lives unbelievably difficult.

Frowning out the window of the van taking him home from his doctor's appointment, Caleb automatically noticed the greening of the pastures. The spring rains had been plentiful this year, thank the gut Lord.

Another reason for thanks was that he'd had an appointment this morning. It had given him a reason to get out of the house early, cutting short any chance of a conversation with Jessie. At the breakfast table, awkwardness had been avoided by the kinder babbling away about the spring program at the Amish school this week. They took it for granted that the whole family would be going. Becky, especially, couldn't wait. She'd been picturing herself in school come fall.

And she'd included Jessie in her imaginings, as if naturally Jessie would be there to pack her lunch and walk her to school on the first day. Jessie had answered her without committing herself, carefully avoiding a glance at him.

Which brought him right back to the problem he'd caused. He'd thought he was being generous, encouraging her to talk about her reasons for coming. He'd felt it was the least he could do, given all the ways she'd helped them.

Maybe he'd even been thinking he should tell her she was welcome in his house for as long as she wanted to stay. But then he'd turned that possibility upside down by giving in to the wave of attraction.

It might be better, safer, if Jessie left. She'd made him realize that he still had longings for a woman to spend his life with, that there might be hope of a normal relationship with someone. But not with Jessie, carrying the baggage of her involvement in Alice's life. That would be a disaster.

His gaze landed on the crutches that lay on the

floor of the van. The doctor had been so pleased with his progress that he'd actually given him permission to start using them a short while each day.

It was thanks to Jessie that he'd made such progress. Once he was on crutches, he'd be on his feet, in a way. On his feet—that was what he'd told Jessie. She could stay until he was on his feet again.

He didn't have time to follow that thought to its difficult conclusion, because they were pulling up to the house.

"Here we are," the driver announced cheerfully, coming around to maneuver the lift that would lower the wheelchair to the ground. "Looks like someone is here to help."

It was Onkel Zeb who'd come out to the van. How long would it take him to start asking questions? Caleb knew perfectly well that Zeb had been aware of the strain between him and Jessie at breakfast. His uncle didn't miss much.

"Back already?" Zeb nodded his thanks to the driver and grabbed the handles of the wheelchair. "What did the doctor say?"

"That I'm doing fine." Caleb took the crutches the driver handed him. "See?"

"Ach, he's not going to let you start using crutches already, is he? He said it would be six weeks, and it's not near that."

"I won't use them all the time," Caleb admitted. He was tempted to skirt what the doctor had actually told him, but he didn't have any desire to do something stupid and ruin all the progress he'd made. "He said I could try them a couple of times a day for a few minutes at a time. Just to see how it will feel to be back on my feet again."

Zeb surveyed him severely. "How many minutes? And where are you allowed to try it? Are you supposed to have help?"

Caleb couldn't suppress a smile. "You sound like a mother hen, ain't so?"

"Mother hen or not, you just answer me." His uncle took up a position in front of the chair, plainly intending that Caleb wouldn't go anywhere until he'd answered.

Caleb sighed. There was no getting away from Onkel Zeb when he was in this mood. "Yah, someone must be with me. No more than fifteen minutes at a time. And only in the house. Satisfied?"

Onkel Zeb gave a crisp nod. "Jessie and I will see there's no cheating, that's certain sure, so don't even think it." He started pushing the chair up the ramp to the back door.

Jessie. Caleb frowned at the crutches he was carrying. If he wanted it, he now had an excuse to send Jessie away. After what happened between them, that might be the smartest thing he could do, no matter how wrong it felt.

Chapter Eleven

"That's enough for now." Jessie put as much steel into her voice as she could, her hand steadying Caleb as he tried to balance on the crutches.

She forced herself not to quail at the angry look he sent her.

"I can judge better than you when I've had enough."

"The doctor is the one who knows better than either of us. According to Onkel Zeb, he told you no more than fifteen minutes at a time." She moved the wheelchair into position behind Caleb.

"Onkel Zeb talks too much," he muttered, but he reached back with one hand for the chair. The crutch slid from under his arm, and she grasped him to ease him into the chair.

"If you overdo, you'll just risk a setback. You don't want that, ain't so?"

For an instant he looked as if he'd snarl at her, but the expression slid away into one more rueful. "Yah, you're right. I get impatient."

"That's only natural." She set the crutches in the corner of the hall, which they'd decided was the best spot for practicing. "But look at how far you've komm just since you got home from the rehab hospital. No one would believe you could do so well in a few short weeks."

He needed the encouragement, she suspected, as well as the cautioning. He was eager to get back on his feet. She feared a big part of that was his determination to get rid of her.

Sure he was settled, she headed back to the kitchen. From the moment he'd gotten his body upright with the help of the crutches, she'd been expecting him to say they could do without her now.

She couldn't fool herself just because he'd seemed so kind the previous night, encouraging her to share her feelings about Alice. That momentary connection between them had been smashed by the wave of longing that seemed to come from nowhere.

Caleb was regretting it today—she'd seen it clearly in the way he'd withdrawn from her at breakfast. Probably he'd consented to let her help with the crutches only because Daniel and Zeb were both out this afternoon, and he had just enough sense to know he couldn't do it alone.

The back door slammed, and Becky and Timothy rushed into the kitchen, Becky carrying a few eggs in a basket.

"Leah is coming," Becky announced.

"And Jacob, too," Timothy added.

"Gut." She gestured to the containers of rhubarb they'd picked that morning. "It's time we were making a batch of jam."

"I'll help," Becky said immediately. "Timmy will play with Jacob, but I'll help."

Jessie hesitated, trying to find the right way to say she'd rather not have a six-year-old around boiling syrup. But Caleb made it unnecessary to disappoint her.

"I need your help this afternoon, Becky. I have to finish sanding those cabinets before Onkel Daniel gets home. I'm counting on you."

Becky sent one regretful glance toward the rhubarb, but the lure of working with her daadi won out. "I like to sand. I'll do it just the way you showed me." She hurried to get behind the wheelchair. "I can help push you up the ramp to the workshop."

"I can, too," Timothy said, obviously determined not to be left out. They headed out the back door, arguing about who should push the chair.

Jessie heard them exchanging greetings with Leah. In a few moments the children's voices faded and Leah came in, smiling.

She set a plastic pail of berries onto the counter. "I have enough strawberries that we can do a few jars of strawberry rhubarb, I figured. Looks as if Caleb is going to keep the kinder out from underfoot while we're making jam. It's just as well, ain't so?"

"There's nothing worse than a burn from boiling sugar syrup," Jessie said. "I've never forgotten the time my mamm and I let Alice help, and she got it on her fingers. I had to chase her across the kitchen to grab her and stick her hand in cold water."

Leah lost no time in starting to wash and cut berries, since Jessie had everything they'd need laid out and the rhubarb already prepared. "I decided I'd help when my mamm was pouring out peanut brittle. That really hurts. Poor Alice. No wonder she lost her head."

She paused, looking at Jessie. "Alice was like a little sister to you. I know that makes it hard to hear how some folks here talk about her."

Jessie nodded, trying not to think of the hurtful words. "I understand how folks feel. After all, they had Caleb and the kinder to care for when she ran off. But it's still difficult." She measured sugar carefully. "I'm grateful that you understand. Alice was..." She stopped, not wanting to say too much.

"Go on," Leah said. "You can talk about her to me, even if Caleb probably isn't ready to hear it."

But Caleb had let her talk last night, hadn't he? Was it possible his bitterness was ebbing?

"Alice was always so bright and cheery. It was like having a ray of sunshine in the house, my daad said. Such a smile she had, and how she'd laugh at the silliest things. You couldn't help but be charmed by her."

"Caleb was, that's certain sure." The pile of berries grew higher in Leah's bowl. "He told me once he'd fallen in love as soon as he set eyes on Alice."

"That's so." Jessie tried to ignore the little pang in her heart at the memory. "He'd traveled out to Ohio for a wedding, and Mamm and Daad offered to house some of the overnight guests. So he came to our place."

"And saw Alice and fell hard," Leah said. She shook her head. "I can't say I think that's a gut way of doing it. Sam and I knew each other all our lives. There wasn't much we didn't know about each other when we married."

"Actually, when he got to the farm, Alice wasn't home. Mamm had me show Caleb around and keep him company." But that wasn't the part Leah wanted to hear. "When we got back to the house, Caleb walked into the kitchen and saw Alice. He stared like he'd never seen a girl before in his life."

She tried to keep her voice light, but the memory was so strong. She'd walked in happy, enjoying Caleb's presence, eager to introduce him to the rest of the family. And then she'd seen him staring dumbstruck at Alice, and all the joy had faded from the day.

She realized Leah was watching her and gave herself a little shake. "The syrup is almost ready. How are the berries coming?"

"About done," Leah said. "Jessie…"

There was a questioning note in her voice, and it was a question Jessie didn't want to answer. She'd never confided her feelings about Caleb to a soul, and she wouldn't now.

"Yah?" She smiled brightly, and Leah seemed to understand.

"I'll scald the jars," she said instead of the question that obviously hovered on her tongue.

They busied themselves with their jobs, and it wasn't until several minutes had passed that Leah spoke again.

"Funny." She glanced around the kitchen. "It must be quite a few years since anyone made jam in here. The last few years, Caleb insisted I take the rhubarb and the berries, so I made jam and brought half over here."

"I noticed someone had stocked the pantry shelves," Jessie said. "I should have known it was you." She poured hot jam carefully into a jar. "I suppose Caleb's mamm did a lot of canning."

"I guess." Leah began wiping jars and capping

them. "I don't remember her all that well, and everything changed once she left." She shook her head. "I've wondered sometimes how the boys would have turned out if she hadn't gone away."

"They were affected, that's certain sure." She thought of Becky and Timothy. She'd just begun to make some headway with them. If only Caleb didn't insist on her going away too soon...

"And then Becky and Timothy went through the same thing," Leah said, her voice heavy. "Almost seems like it runs in families, though I guess that's silly. Still, they've been much better since you've been here."

"I hope I can make a difference for them."

Leah eyed her, speculation in her face. "Maybe you'll be here for good. It's time Caleb gave those kinder a mother and himself a wife."

Heat flooded Jessie's face. "Don't matchmake, please, Leah. It's impossible."

"Why?" Leah didn't seem ready to give up her idea. "Nobody could love those kinder more than you do, and it's plain you care about Caleb. So just tell me why not."

"I can't. It would be wrong." She felt as if she couldn't breathe. "I let Alice down. I wasn't there when Alice needed me. It would be wrong to take her place."

"Nonsense," Leah said robustly. "Alice was a grown woman who made her own choices. That's no reason you and Caleb and the kinder should suffer."

All Jessie could do was shake her head. After those moments when they'd felt the strength of the attraction between them, Caleb probably felt just as guilty as she did. No matter what she might wish, Alice would always stand between them.

By the time he spotted Daniel's buggy pulling up to the barn, Caleb had sent the kinder out to play while he finished the cabinets. The soothing, repetitive nature of the work gave him plenty of time to think. Unfortunately, his thoughts just kept going around in circles.

One part of him kept saying that now that he was better, he had a good excuse for sending Jessie back to Ohio. And a good reason, too, given the way he'd responded to her last night. But his conscience insisted that it would be wrong to send her away just because he hadn't been able to control his desires. Her reason for coming was admirable, even if he thought she was overreacting with her guilt.

Daniel came in, arms full. He stacked supplies on one of the work tables and looked over Caleb's shoulder. "You've got a lot finished. Denke, Caleb. I don't see how I'd be able to do this job without your help."

Caleb shrugged off his thanks. "You should think of bringing in an apprentice once I'm back to work. Especially if this job leads to more. Once this client's neighbors see your work, you may have more than you can handle."

Daniel seemed unimpressed. "Sometimes I think they just want to say their cabinets are Amish-made."

"As long as they hire you, what difference does it make?" Caleb studied his brother's face, wondering at the slight frown he wore. "You and I might know that being Amish doesn't automatically make you a fine craftsman, but that's what you are."

"I guess so." Daniel's face relaxed in a smile. "I'm too picky. I want them to hire me because I'm good, not because I'm Amish."

"So you're both. They win both ways." He was relieved to see the smile. People who didn't know his brother well might have been fooled by his carefree exterior, but Caleb knew how conscientious he was. Daniel would always do his best, no matter what it cost him.

Daniel focused on organizing the supplies he'd brought in, and Caleb went back to putting the final touches on the cabinets. Even though he didn't come by the work naturally like Daniel, it was still a pleasure to feel the wood grow smooth and silky under his hand. They worked together in comfortable silence.

Then Daniel looked at him with a question in his face. "You didn't tell me about the crutches. Did you try them out earlier, or were you waiting for me to get home?"

"Already done," Caleb said. "Jessie helped me." He considered. "I'd say it went pretty well for the first time. Made me feel normal again to be standing and moving."

"Sehr gut." Daniel hesitated. "You're not going back to using that for an excuse to get rid of Jessie so soon, are you?"

Caleb evaded his eyes. "I don't know. I'll maybe soon be well enough we could just have someone in for a few hours a day to watch the kinder, ain't so?"

"No." Daniel leaned against the workbench, frowning. "Not if you mean to subject us to Onkel Zeb's cooking again."

"Do you ever think of anything but your stomach?"

Caleb tried to keep his voice light. He didn't want to talk about Jessie leaving. He was already having enough trouble with the idea.

"It's important," Daniel protested. "Besides, Jessie's wonderful gut with the kinder. I'm not saying it's like having a mamm of their own, but I don't know who'd be any better. Do you?"

Caleb gritted his teeth at the direct question. It hit too close to the bone. "Why don't you think about getting married to some nice girl? Becky and Timothy would love to have an aunt."

Daniel turned away. "Just haven't run across the right one, that's all."

"Is it?" Caleb felt a sudden longing to see someone in the family make a success of love. "Are you sure it's not because of…well, because of Mamm? And because of the mess I made of marriage? You shouldn't give up on the idea because of that."

"I could tell you the same thing, ain't so?" His brother's quick gaze challenged him. "Seems to me you're the one who's given up on being happy."

The words seemed to hang in the quiet room between them. Caleb clamped his lips together. He wasn't going to respond. Not now. Maybe not ever.

Chapter Twelve

Nothing was any pleasanter than having the family sitting together in the living room as the sun slipped behind the ridge. Jessie paused in her mending to let her gaze rest on Caleb, relaxed in the easy chair he'd insisted on moving to from the wheelchair. He had a newspaper in his hands, but he looked over it at Timothy and Becky, playing more or less quietly together on the floor.

Jessie could understand his insistence on getting out of the wheelchair. Every small step he took toward recovery was important to him, even if it was as simple as sitting in his usual seat.

Funny how quickly this rocker had become hers. Onkel Zeb had gone automatically to the end of the sofa, pushing her mending basket over next to her as she reached for it.

Daniel had disappeared in the direction of his workshop after the chores were done, saying he wanted to get his materials ready for the next day. He'd shaken his head, smiling a little, when both his uncle and his brother offered to help.

"I want to plan the work out in my head," he'd said. "You'll just be a distraction."

That was probably the best way he could have picked to dissuade Caleb from going out with him. Caleb had thrown himself into work in the shop, no doubt from his need to repay Daniel for all the farm work he was doing. That determination was a measure of Caleb's personality, she suspected. He hated being dependent more than anyone she'd ever known.

Perhaps the accident was God's way of confronting Caleb with that, but she knew he wouldn't want to hear it.

Following his gaze to the two children, she found herself smiling. Timothy had reached the point of taking her presence as a fact of life, and it never seemed to occur to him that she wouldn't always be there.

As for Becky...well, Jessie couldn't entirely suppress a sigh. Becky had been much more cooperative lately, and any resentment she might have felt over Jessie's presence seemed to have disappeared that day that she'd sobbed her heart out and Jessie had comforted her.

But Becky still wasn't the happy, carefree little girl she was meant to be. She accepted Jessie, but the closeness Jessie longed for hadn't been forthcoming.

How could she reach the child and make a difference to her if Becky didn't let her guard down? They needed a situation that would encourage Becky to talk, and Jessie hadn't yet found it. She thought longingly of the hours she and her mamm had spent chatting about anything and everything while they washed the dishes each evening. But if she tried to engage

Becky that way, Timothy would be right there, determined not to be left out.

She glanced down at the sewing in her lap and remembered her thought about introducing Becky to quilting. The quilt squares she'd cut were still in her basket, but she and the kinder had been busy with other things and it had slipped her mind. Maybe now was the time to introduce it.

As she tucked the mending away and began taking out the quilting squares, Becky crossed the room to her daad. "Daadi, you didn't forget going to the school tomorrow, did you?"

"No, for sure I didn't." Caleb put the paper down. "You'll be going to school every day come September. We'll go so we can all get a gut look at it."

Timothy, overhearing, pouted. "I want to go to school, too."

"You'll see the program tomorrow," Jessie reminded him. "Then you can imagine what it's like when Becky is there."

"I wish I was older," he declared, but the pout receded.

Onkel Zeb chuckled. "You won't feel that way in a few more years, young Timothy."

Timothy looked a little puzzled at that, but he noticed the patches Jessie was laying out on her lap, and that distracted him.

"What are those, Cousin Jessie?" He poked at a patch with one finger.

"These are the quilt squares. Remember? I showed you some before, and you tried sewing. When these are all stitched together, they'll make a small quilt, just big enough for a doll or a teddy bear. I'm trying to see which patches will look best next to each other."

"Can't you just make them all the same?" he asked.

"Silly," Becky said, showing off her experience. "Quilts always have different colors on each patch."

"I guess they wouldn't have to, but they're prettier this way," Jessie said, peacemaking. "It's called a nine-patch, because I'll put one in the middle and eight around it." She laid out a sample on her skirt. "Then you sew them together for the quilt."

Becky reached out tentatively and rearranged one of the squares. Encouraged, Jessie smiled at the child. "Do you want to pick out some squares, Becky? I have lots of them. You'll stitch them together just like you sewed that practice piece the other night."

Becky hesitated, and Jessie held her breath, hoping she hadn't sounded too eager. Then Becky nodded.

Jessie scooped the rest of the fabric squares from the basket and fanned them out. "Which ones would you put together?"

Timothy started to reach in front of Becky for a square, but Onkel Zeb called his name.

"Timothy, komm over here. Let's see if I remember how to make a lamb from a piece of wood."

Timmy scrambled over to his great-onkel, hanging on him as he got a penknife out. Jessie looked her thanks at him. Zeb, at least, understood what she was trying to do.

Becky quickly got into the idea of laying out the squares into a pattern, and Jessie smiled at the intent look on Becky's face. When she concentrated so hard, she very much resembled her daadi. Jessie glanced at Caleb and found him watching her. His face softened into a smile, and for a long moment they just looked at each other.

Then she felt the heat rising in her cheeks and focused on the fabric again. What did that stare mean, if anything?

"How about these two together?" She put a brown square against a black one.

Becky wrinkled up her nose. "Too dark," she said decidedly. "Maybe this." She picked up a rose-colored piece and laid it out next to the black.

"Very nice." Jessie felt a slight inward twinge. That rose piece was from a dress Alice had in her early teens. She'd looked like a flower in it.

Finally the squares were arranged to Becky's satisfaction. "Now we sew them together, ain't so?"

Jessie nodded. "I'll thread a couple of needles," she said, taking out the spool. "Why don't you match up the edges of two squares so they're just right?"

Becky pulled a stool over next to Jessie and picked up two of the squares. Her forehead wrinkled into a frown of concentration as she focused on matching them exactly. Like her daadi, she wanted to do everything perfectly.

"Now we start to stitch them together." Jessie showed Becky how to move the needle, picking up a small stitch. "It will be hard at first to sew a straight line, but it will get easier with practice."

Becky managed to get two stitches more or less in place before she pricked her finger and stopped to suck on it. She eyed Jessie. "You learned to sew when you were my age, ain't so?"

"Yah, that's right. My mamm taught me. I used to stick myself sometimes, too." She smiled at the memory. "My mamm said that my fingers would get better long before the nine-patch was finished. And she was right."

Becky stuck her needle in the fabric again. "Did you make one like this?"

"Yah, but different colors. It was in my doll cradle for a long time. Alice made one for her bear, I remember."

She was smiling until she saw the rigid look come over Becky's face. How foolish of her—she'd said the one thing that might turn Becky against the idea of quilting. But the girl couldn't go through life refusing to do anything her mother had done, could she?

Becky put the sewing down carefully and got up from the stool. "I don't want to sew anymore now." She went to Onkel Zeb, seeming instantly absorbed in what he was doing.

Frustrated, Jessie frowned at Caleb. Hadn't he said he'd work on showing Becky it was okay to be like her mammi? As far as she could tell, he'd never bothered to do it.

Caleb returned her look with one that was half ashamed and half stubborn. She ought to have been angry, but instead she felt only sorrow. Helplessness. What would break this cycle of blame and guilt that kept Caleb and his children trapped in this difficult place?

Caleb grasped the arms of the wheelchair as Onkel Zeb moved him into place at the rear of the schoolroom, Jessie following with the children. Several of Caleb's friends and neighbors got up, greeting him, making room on the benches for everyone.

He'd wanted to come to the school program on crutches, but Zeb had talked him out of it, reasoning that it would be hard to maneuver in the crowded room without tripping someone. He'd been right, that was certain sure. It looked as if the whole church was here. Everyone wanted to see the scholars put on their program—one of the few times Amish children performed for others, since that idea smacked of being prideful.

The one-room school hadn't changed, it seemed, since he'd been a scholar here. The alphabet still marched across the wall over the top of the chalkboard. Someone had put a Wilkom Friends sign on the board, decorated with flowers in colored chalk.

Becky had wiggled her way next to him on the end of the bench, and now she pulled at his arm. "Where will I sit when I'm a scholar?"

Putting his arm around her, he pointed to the small desks at the front of the room. "You'll be right up there. Teacher Mary wants the first-graders up front so she can help them."

His daughter stood to scan the front row of desks, now occupied by the schoolchildren who were waiting and eager to begin. "I want that one, on the end," she whispered in his ear.

"Maybe you'll be there, maybe not. It's Teacher Mary who decides."

Becky looked slightly mutinous for a moment, but then she nodded and relapsed into silence, her small face grave.

What had happened to the bright, sunny child she used to be? His conscience struck him a blow, and he glanced at Jessie. She seemed to know.

They hadn't spoken about last night. In fact, Jessie seemed determined to ignore the incident.

Not so Onkel Zeb. He'd had plenty to say once he got Caleb alone. And Caleb knew he was right. It was his responsibility to help his daughter come to terms with what her mother had done. He'd told Jessie he would. But when it came right down to it, he hadn't been able to find the words.

Fortunately, the program started before he tied himself in too many knots trying to rationalize his failure. No one could think of anything else while the young scholars were saying their pieces and singing their songs.

He had to smile, remembering the school programs of his youth. There was the year he'd completely forgotten his lines and stood there, turning red, until the teacher had prompted him. To say nothing of the time Aaron had knocked over a whole display of posters by backing into it.

Timmy, seated on Jessie's lap so he could see better, was wiggling, but Becky sat rapt, totally engaged in every line. Her lips moved silently along with the songs.

Caleb smiled, watching her, and found himself automatically looking at Jessie, wanting to share the moment with her. She was looking at Becky, as well, but then she glanced at him. Her serene face curved in a smile, and it was hard to look away. How could it be that he was communicating wordlessly with her?

His gaze dropped. He didn't want to feel that comfortable with her. It was yet another reminder that he had to move forward, and he didn't know how.

When the program ended, everyone began moving

outside for the picnic and games that always closed out the school year. The chatter of the crowd was immediate, and he was kept busy answering questions about his health.

Willing hands lifted the chair down the single step out of the white frame schoolhouse, and Zeb pushed Caleb toward the picnic tables where the scholars' mothers were busy putting out food. He spotted Jessie taking the kinder to the table and knew he didn't have to worry about them. Jessie would take care of them.

Zeb parked him next to a group of men. "You stay here and catch up on all the news. I'll bring you a plate."

"No need to pile it into a mountain," Caleb called after his uncle. Zeb seemed to think he would recover faster if he was stuffed with food. Just like an Amish mother, he was.

Caleb found it rejuvenating to join in the talk of the weather, the crops, who was planting what, who'd increased his dairy herd and who was having trouble with the cooperative dairy. The ordinary topics of life in a farming community were of vital interest to no one but the folks who lived there. To them, such things were crucial, and just chatting with the others made him feel a part of it again.

The group dispersed as they finished eating, some to join the ball game that was starting, others to watch and cheer.

"Looks like the kinder are done eating," Zeb observed, nodding at Becky and Timothy, who were running toward the swings.

Caleb's gaze lingered on Becky. For once she was laughing, distracted from her troubles. She ought to have been that way all the time. He glanced at Zeb and found his uncle watching him.

"Yah, all right." Caleb frowned at him. "I know what you're thinking. And you're right. I have to try harder with Becky. It's just…difficult."

Zeb took a breath before he spoke, a sure sign he was weighing his words. "You're finding it hard."

"I'm finding it impossible," Caleb said flatly. "Jessie thinks I ought to be able to talk normally about Alice to the kinder, and I can't. It keeps coming out stiff."

"You think maybe that's because you haven't really forgiven her yet?"

Caleb smacked his palms on the arms of the chair. "I've tried. The gut Lord knows I've tried. I think I've done it, and then the anger and resentment pop back up again."

"Ach, Caleb, what do you expect? That's what forgiveness is like. If you found it easy, it surely wouldn't be real. You forgive, and then the next day when the feeling comes up again, you forgive again. One day you'll know that this time it will stick."

"That's what Jessie says. I hope you're both right," he muttered with no great confidence.

His uncle gave him a stern look. "You know what to do. Take it to the Lord. He will help you. And when you understand what the next step is, take it. Whether you want to or not."

Caleb nodded, feeling the reluctance drag at him. Yah, he knew what the next steps were. To apologize to Jessie. And then to speak naturally about Alice to his daughter.

Muttering that he was getting some coffee, he maneuvered the chair toward the table where he'd last seen Jessie.

The wheels moved quietly over the grass, newly mown for the event, and probably the bishop's wife and her daughter-in-law didn't hear his approach.

"I saw how they looked at each other," Ethel Braun was saying. "They should be ashamed of themselves."

"Maybe you misunderstood..." the daughter-in-law began timidly.

"I did not! I'd never have thought it of Caleb. That woman is out to trap him into marriage just like her cousin did, and we all know how badly that turned out."

He could back up silently. Pretend he hadn't heard anything. Nobody wanted to start an argument with the bishop's wife. Bishop Thomas himself was kind and reasonable. What he'd done to deserve a woman with such a sharp tongue, nobody knew.

But he couldn't let it go. He knew how much killing a rumor of that sort took. If he didn't scotch it today, half the county would be wondering tomorrow. Jessie didn't deserve that.

"Excuse me." *Be polite*, he told himself. *No matter what you're thinking.*

The two of them swung around. The younger woman went scarlet when she saw him. But the bishop's wife just looked more sharp-featured than ever.

"Caleb." For a moment he thought she was going to ignore the whole thing, but then she gave a short nod. "I suppose you heard what I said. I suppose I hurt your feelings, but..."

"I'm not easily hurt by gossip," he said bluntly,

forgetting his resolve. "But Cousin Jessie has done nothing, and it's not right to spread rumors about her."

Faint, unbecoming color stained her thin cheeks. "Are you accusing me of being a blabbermaul?"

If the shoe fits, he thought but didn't say.

"When you talk that way about an innocent woman, what am I to think? Jessie has been nothing but kind in helping my kinder and taking care of the house during this difficult time." He was building up a head of steam. He should have stopped, but he couldn't. "She knew she would be facing rejection by coming here, but she came, anyway."

She came, knowing what she'd have to contend with, and he hadn't been much help. It was time he made a fresh start.

He spun the chair around and froze. Jessie stood there, and it was obvious she'd heard the whole thing.

Chapter Thirteen

Jessie started down the stairs to the living room that evening after she'd gotten everything ready for putting the kinder to bed. She stopped abruptly when Caleb's voice reached her.

"...didn't you want to make a quilt with Cousin Jessie? I thought it would be nice to do."

Jessie froze, pressing her hands against the wall as she strained to hear what reply Becky might make.

"I don't know," Becky mumbled. "I just didn't want to."

Caleb cleared his throat as if talking had become difficult. "You know, your mamm was really good at sewing things. I think you would be, too."

If only Jessie could see their faces. Then she might know what they were thinking and how Becky was reacting. But she was afraid to move for fear of interrupting them.

Caleb was actually doing what she'd hoped. She could hardly believe he was able to speak that way to Becky. True, he didn't sound very comfortable, but at least he was trying.

"I don't know," Becky said again, and Jessie could imagine the confusion she must feel. Her mother hadn't been spoken of in this house for what would seem a long time to a child.

"Maybe you could ask Cousin Jessie to show you a little more about quilting before you decide you don't like it," Onkel Zeb suggested.

"Yah, that's a gut idea." Caleb sounded relieved at the helpful interruption.

"I'd like a doll quilt," Daniel said. "Make me one."

Becky giggled, and Jessie decided it was safe to go the rest of the way down. "And what would you do with a doll quilt?" she asked, keeping her voice light. "It would only cover one of your hands."

"Or one foot," Becky said, her face alight.

"Wrong, both of you." Daniel swung Becky up toward the ceiling, gave her a hug and set her down again. "I'd wrap it around my coffee thermos to keep it hot when I go to work." He shot a glance at Onkel Zeb. "Ready to help me load those cabinets on the buggy?"

"Sure thing. You'll want to put some padding between them. And a tarp on top to protect them overnight."

"Sounds gut. I want to make an early start tomorrow." Daniel ruffled Timothy's hair. "About bedtime for you, ain't so? I'll see you in the morning."

Timothy dropped a wooden horse in the toy box and flung his arms around Daniel in a hug. "See you in the morning," he echoed.

There was a little spell of silence when the two men had gone. Jessie smiled at the children. "I think it's time to tell Daadi good-night now. Don't you?"

Timothy shoved the toy box against the wall and went to hug his daadi. But Becky hesitated, looking at Jessie. "Can we sew a little bit more tomorrow?"

It took an effort to hide her pleasure. "For sure. I'd like that."

Apparently satisfied, Becky nodded before she trotted over to tell Caleb good-night. Above the child's head, Jessie's gaze met Caleb's. *Thank you.* She mouthed the words, and Caleb nodded. Unable to stop smiling, she walked up the stairs with Becky while Timothy scurried up ahead of them.

The usual routine of putting the children to bed seemed doubly precious to Jessie that night. The kinder had grown so dear to her. Just the fact that Caleb was supporting her made her feel more a part of the family, so much so that she couldn't bear the thought of leaving.

Maybe that was what Mamm had been thinking when she'd worried about Jessie coming here. That she'd give her heart away and not be able to take it back.

Jessie sat down on Timothy's bed, and he and Becky hopped up on either side of her. She snuggled them close. "What kind of story will it be tonight?"

"A story about a rabbit," Timothy said quickly. He'd been engrossed in the story of Peter Rabbit lately.

"Peter Rabbit?" she suggested. "Benjamin Bunny?"

"We already heard those," Becky said. "Tell us a story about an Amish girl who had a rabbit."

Becky seemed to like making her use her imagination when it came to bedtime stories. "All right, but you'll have to help me."

Thinking quickly, Jessie began a story that relied a

little on the fact that her cousin had once raised rabbits. She encouraged the children to fill in details of color and place, loving the way their imaginations caught hold.

When the story had wound its way to the end, with the bunny safely back in his hutch after his adventures, she tucked them in, bending over Timmy for one of his throttling hugs. When she went to Becky she paused, as always, for any sign that an embrace would be welcome. She found Becky looking up at her solemnly.

"Cousin Jessie, am I like my mammi?" It was said in a very small voice.

Jessie's heart ached. What was the right answer to that question?

"You're like your mammi in some ways, and like your daadi in others," she said. "Parts of each, all mixed up to make a special Becky."

Apparently it was the correct response. Becky smiled and lifted her head for a good-night kiss, putting her arms around Jessie's neck in a long hug.

Jessie went back down the stairs slowly, knowing that when she reached the living room, she and Caleb would be alone. They had to talk about what the bishop's wife had said, didn't they? The fear that he'd think she was trying to trap him nagged at her. She had to face it, but what she really wanted was to go straight to the walkway that led to the daadi haus and hibernate there until morning.

But that would be cowardly. So she walked into the living room, knowing that Caleb would be waiting for her and not looking forward to it any more than she was.

She began to talk when she entered the room, afraid she'd panic if she waited any longer. "Caleb, about what happened at the school…"

"I'm sorry," he said abruptly. His jaw was like iron.

"Sorry for what? You didn't do anything."

"I don't think I honestly realized the harm I was doing by how I thought about…about Alice. I thought it was my own business. But it must have been obvious to everyone else in the community."

She took the chair next to him. "You had every right to be angry with Alice, Caleb. I know that better than anyone."

"Yah. But I hardly considered how folks would act toward you because of it."

"They haven't all been like the bishop's wife," she hurried to assure him. "Leah has been kindness itself, and many others have been friendly."

That didn't seem to make him feel any better. "I should have thought. Just like I should have seen what was happening with my Becky." He shook his head and seemed to fight for control. "Why, Jessie? Why did Alice act as she did? Why couldn't she be happy with the life we had?"

Her throat was tight with pain, and she struggled to speak. "I don't know. But I thought from the beginning that she was too young. She hadn't…hadn't settled yet, inside herself. It was like she was always looking for a place to belong."

Caleb turned a tortured face to her. "That's what I wanted to give her."

"I know. You did your best. We did, too. From the time her mamm died, she was like one of our own, but…"

"But you failed. I failed, too."

She put her hand on his arm, helpless to comfort him. "We did our best. Somehow what we offered was never enough to fill the empty place inside her."

"No." Caleb sucked in a deep breath, and some of the tension seemed to seep out. "When she came back, I thought at first she was sorry. That she wanted to make up for what she'd done. But I guess she just wanted a place to die."

On that subject, at least, she could reassure him. But it meant revealing things she'd never intended to say.

She pressed her fingers against her temples. "It's not…not quite that way. Really. I offered to have her. We could have moved into the daadi haus at my brother's. I would have taken care of her." She paused, trying to find the truth of her emotions at that painful time. "I should have tried harder. Maybe she knew how angry I was with her, even though I tried to forgive."

"Forgiving isn't easy." He shook his head. "It wasn't your fault."

They would each have to carry their own burden in that regard, it seemed.

"There's more," she said. "When Alice was here at the end, she wrote to me. She hadn't been writing regularly for a long time, but she did then. She…she said she came back because she hoped to put things right in the little time she had left. So, you see…"

His fingers tightened painfully around her wrist. "She wrote? You have a letter she wrote when she was dying?"

She nodded, helpless to do otherwise.

"Why haven't you shown me?" He clamped his mouth closed for a moment. "Never mind. I wouldn't give you a chance, would I?"

"No. And I didn't want to hurt you."

"Hurt me?" He said it as if it sounded ridiculous. "I want to see it. I must see it."

She looked at him for a long moment, not sure if this was wise. But what else could she do, now that he knew?

She nodded, rising. "I'll get it." She looked down at his hand, still taut around her wrist.

He grimaced, letting go. "Sorry," he muttered.

"It's nothing." She turned, heading for the kitchen and the door that led to the daadi haus, a sense of dread weighing on her heart. Would knowing what Alice wrote hurt him? Or heal him?

Caleb found he was gripping the arms of the wheelchair so tightly that his fingers were white. He relaxed them deliberately, one by one, trying not to think of anything else.

His thoughts didn't cooperate, racing ahead to what Alice might have written. Jessie had so clearly not wanted to show him. But Jessie, he'd begun to see, had a tender heart under her practical exterior. She couldn't bear to hurt anyone.

Did she imagine anything could be worse than the hurt he'd already endured? It was better to know everything.

He heard the door, and then Jessie's footsteps sounded lightly in the kitchen. He waited, praying that Onkel Zeb and Daniel wouldn't return too soon. For this he needed privacy.

He watched her come through the doorway and turn toward him. The letter was in her hand, and he couldn't tear his gaze away.

It was only a couple of seconds, but it seemed forever until she held the envelope out and sank into the chair next to him.

Now that he had it, he couldn't seem to muster the courage to look at it. He turned it over and over in his hands. "How is it I knew nothing about her writing to you?"

"I don't know."

"I wouldn't have stopped her from writing to you." The words were laced with bitterness. Was that what Alice had thought of him toward the end? That he'd have been mean enough to suppress her letters?

"I know you wouldn't. I'm sure she knew that, as well. Maybe she didn't want to talk about it."

"To me," he added to her words. "Zeb wrote the address. I know his writing."

"Does it matter?" Jessie's tone was gentle. "She'd have known how busy you were, and I'm sure things were strained enough already. It would have been natural to ask Onkel Zeb to do it."

"I guess." He knew what he was doing. He was delaying the moment when he'd actually have to read Alice's words. Being a coward.

The thought propelled him forward, and he opened the envelope.

The notepaper was worn and creased as if Jessie had read it time and again. He unfolded it and began to read.

You were right, Jessie, like always. I shouldn't have come here. I thought I could do some good.

No, I promised I wouldn't lie to myself anymore. I wanted forgiveness for myself. Selfish, I guess, but I did think it might help Caleb and the children.

I was wrong. Caleb can't forgive me. Oh, he says the words, but I can see the bitterness in his heart. I should know. I put it there. He can't forgive, and I'm only hurting the children by letting them see me this way. It's not so bad for Timmy. He's just a baby, and he'll forget.

But Becky...dear Jessie, please do what you can to help my little daughter. Don't let her grow up bitter and lonely.

I'm always asking things of you, ain't so? But never anything as important as this. Please, Jessie. I pray that you can do what I can't.

Don't grieve too much for me. It was only when I faced death that I knew what a mess I'd made of living. But I have confessed and asked the good Lord for forgiveness. I rest on His promise to forgive.

Try to remember the silly little cousin who always wanted to be like you, and let the rest slip away to dust.

Caleb's eyes stung with salty tears, and he closed them tightly, struggling to gain control as he let the letter drop in his lap. Poor Alice. Poor, foolish Alice. She had grabbed for what she thought she wanted, only to find it turn to ashes.

"All she asked of me was forgiveness." He struggled to get the words out. "But I couldn't give it." He slammed his fist on the arm of the chair as if that would help.

"Don't, Caleb." Jessie took his tight fist in her hand. "You did your best. That's all anyone can do."

He turned blindly toward her, fighting not to give way. "If only..."

"I know."

Jessie put her hand tentatively on his back, the way she would comfort one of the children. He leaned against her arm as if it were the most natural thing in the world. He could feel the caring flow from her to him, soothing his battered heart.

"There are so many things I could have done better." Speech came more easily now. "Words I could have spoken. Acceptance I could have shown."

"The same is true for me. I keep thinking there was something more I could have done to keep her from coming back here when she was dying. It would have spared you and the kinder so much."

"Don't think that." He enclosed her hand in both of his. "None of it was your fault. The responsibility was mine. I took the vows, not you. I am to blame."

"Ach, Caleb, it's a gut thing the Lord knows we're only human. We all make mistakes. Alice, too. She knew that. Didn't you see what she said? She confessed and accepted God's forgiveness. We must do the same."

"Onkel Zeb told..." He paused, not sure he wanted to go on. But who should he say it to but Jessie, who was so deeply involved? "He told me I was passing my doubts and lack of trust on to the next generation. Folks already say the King boys don't fare well in love. If I didn't change, one day they'd be saying that about Becky and Timothy, too."

Maybe he hoped she'd deny that, but she didn't. "Onkel Zeb is a wise man," she said softly. "But you have already begun to make that right, ain't so?"

"Only because you've been here to guide me." He managed a rueful smile. "With me fighting you every step of the way."

"Not as bad as that," she said. "Becky is more open already, thanks to you."

He shook his head. "Not me. You. If we have changed, it's because of you, Jessie."

He looked into her eyes and seemed to become lost in their depths. He leaned toward her, longing filling him. Not for comfort this time, but for her. For Jessie herself.

He touched her cheek, feeling the smooth skin beneath his fingers. She flushed, her lips trembling just a little. And then he leaned across the barrier of the wheelchair arm and kissed her.

It was a long, slow kiss, gentle at first but deepening as he felt her response. He inhaled the sweet, feminine scent of her, heard her breathing quicken and felt her lips warm. Her hand touched his nape tentatively, then more surely as she leaned into his kiss. The world seemed to narrow until it encompassed only the two of them.

Slowly, reluctantly, she drew back. "I don't… I'm not sure. Is this right, for me to care about you this way?"

He put his finger across her lips. "You have been so intent on making the rest of us free to move ahead.

Now you have to do the same for yourself. It can't be wrong to hope for a better future, can it?"

He saw the doubt ebb from her face, to be replaced by the gentle smile he loved.

"No. Hope is never wrong."

Chapter Fourteen

It was still dark in the kitchen when Jessie began getting breakfast ready, but the sky was lightening in the east, and it would soon be day. Dairy farmers got up early. That was part of the business, and this morning Caleb had insisted on going out to the barn with the other men. There might not be much he could do, but he was determined to take another step toward normal life.

A smile touched Jessie's lips. Once, normal had meant getting rid of her. Now...now it meant something much different.

She cautioned herself not to expect too much, but it was impossible. Caleb wouldn't kiss her that way unless he intended marriage. They weren't teenagers, smooching with one after another on the way to finding a life partner. At their age, a person didn't get involved without it being serious.

She must convince Caleb that they couldn't rush into anything. They'd have to give the children time. But...

Daniel came in, bringing a blast of chill early

morning air with him, and gave her a sharp look. "What are you smiling about?"

"I'm not," she said, schooling her face to her usual calm.

"Sure you were. What's up?" He helped himself to a mug of coffee and leaned against the counter to drink it.

She shrugged, thinking she'd have to be more careful if she didn't want everyone talking about her and Caleb. "Just thinking about plans for the day, I guess. I've filled a thermos with coffee for you, and your lunch is packed. Do you have time for breakfast, or should I wrap something up?"

Daniel glanced at the clock and straightened. "I'd better get going. Just give me a couple pieces of the shoofly pie. That'll be enough."

Nodding, Jessie wrapped up half the pie, knowing how Daniel liked to eat, even though it never showed on his lean frame. He grabbed lunch pail, thermos and the bag into which she'd put the shoofly pie.

"Denke, Jessie. I'll have it on the way to the job."

He went out, the door banging behind him. She heard him exchange a few words with the others, so they must be on their way in. She began dishing up oatmeal from the pot on the stove as the kinder thudded their way down the stairs.

Breakfast was a time for chatter about what the day would hold. Jessie tried resolutely to keep from catching Caleb's gaze, but every time she glanced at him, he was watching her with a warmth in his face that was a sure signal to anyone studying him. She'd warn him to be more careful.

She was on pins and needles throughout the meal,

sure he was going to give them away. Somehow they got through without it happening, although she did think Onkel Zeb was looking at them a little oddly.

At last the kitchen emptied out except for her and Caleb. He shoved his chair toward her.

"We're finally alone. I thought they'd never finish breakfast." He caught her hand.

She sent a quick look around to be sure they were really alone. "Ach, Caleb, you have to be more careful. I'm sure Onkel Zeb thought something was going on, the way you kept looking at me."

"But I want to look at you, my Jessie." He drew her down for a quick kiss. "It's a good morning when we're together. Ain't so?"

"Yah." She cupped his cheek with her hand for a moment. "But I mean it about being careful not to let anyone suspect our feelings."

"Why not? Why not just let them know that we're going to marry?"

"Are we?" she asked, smiling in spite of her efforts to stay sober.

"Of course we are. If you go around kissing men the way you kissed me without marriage in mind, all I can say is that I'm surprised at you."

"Silly. I don't go around kissing anyone. Except you," she added. She yanked her mind away from the joy of joking with him. "But it's best if we don't let anyone in on it, at least not yet." She could see the objection forming in his thoughts and hurried on. "For the children's sake, Caleb. We should move gradually. They'll need time to adjust."

"We doubtless won't convince anyone to marry us

until fall," he pointed out, reminding her of the traditional season for weddings. "Isn't that time to adjust?"

"Yah, but I want to be positive sure that Becky has accepted me before expecting her to think of me as your future wife."

"And her mother," Caleb added. "They'll be happy. Why wouldn't they be? But I guess you're right. We don't want any setbacks now, that's for sure."

"Denke, Caleb. I knew you'd understand."

He smiled. "So long as you understand that I'll need to snatch a kiss now and then. Just to keep me going."

"I think we can manage that," she said gravely, while her eyes danced.

He lifted her hand to his lips and dropped a light kiss on it. "So much to look forward to. Soon I'll trade this big cast in for a smaller one, I'll be able to do more, and we'll be busy making plans for our marriage. I feel as if I've come out from under a dark cloud."

"I know. I feel it, too."

"Then come here and give me a kiss before everyone comes back again." He drew her down, cradling her face in his hands. "One to last through the morning," he said, kissing her lightly. "And another…"

Something…some sound…had her turning to look around.

"What's wrong?" Caleb sobered at once.

"I…nothing, I guess. I thought I heard something."

"Just the house making noises as it settles," he said, and he pulled her back to him for a long, satisfying kiss.

* * *

Caleb, trying to sweep the workshop floor, decided that sweeping was best done by someone who had two feet to stand on. It was difficult to manipulate the broom and impossible to manage the dustpan from a wheelchair.

He glared at the heavy cast on his leg. He'd be wonderful glad to be rid of it. Maybe, when he went to have it checked tomorrow, they'd decide he could make do with the small one that would let him be more mobile.

Leaning back in the chair, he gave himself up to thoughts of the future. The initial euphoria he'd felt last night when he'd realized he loved Jessie had already subsided to a quiet contentment. That was as it should be, wasn't it?

When he'd met Alice, he'd tumbled into love without a single sensible thought in his head. They'd hurried into marriage because they couldn't bear to be parted, and probably because he'd feared losing this wondrous thing that had happened to him.

How long had it taken to see that they hadn't known each other at all? By the time they did, it was too late.

Everything was different with Jessie. Not less, only different. He'd moved slowly from distrust to wariness, then to cautious acceptance and finally to love. It had been so gradual that he almost didn't realize it was happening until he'd known, for certain sure, that what he felt was love.

He'd rebelled at first at not sharing their happiness with everyone right away, but probably Jessie was right. They needed to do what was best for the kinder. They'd be happy, wouldn't they? They already loved Jessie.

But it was worth taking their time so it was the right moment to tell them. When they did...

The door rattled, and Onkel Zeb came in on a wave of warm air filled with the scent of spring. "Getting stuffy in here, ain't so? Let's see if I can get one of these windows open." He began wrestling with the front window.

"Let me help." Caleb moved the wheelchair into position, and together they managed to push the balky window up. "That's better. Smells like spring, ain't so?"

Zeb nodded. "Soon it'll be summer. The corn we planted is showing green already."

"Gut." Caleb smacked the arms of the chair. "The sooner I get out of this, the better."

"I'm thinking we should tell Thomas we'll keep him on until fall, at least. He'd be glad to know his steady work will go on." Zeb glanced around the shop. "Daniel had best get moving on finding an apprentice. He'll need someone soon."

"Any ideas?" Caleb pushed away from the window, reflecting that Onkel Zeb was never happier than when he was taking care of them.

"I hear tell that Zeke Esch's second boy, Eli, is wonderful gut with his hands. Zeke says he likes working with wood. Seems to me he'd be a good possibility. Zeke would like to see the boy settled in a trade."

Caleb smiled. Things would probably work out just the way Onkel Zeb had in mind. They usually did.

The future was falling into a new pattern, it seemed. Not bad, just different.

He realized that his uncle was studying his face. "Anything you want to tell me?" Zeb asked.

"What makes you say that?" Caleb parried, playing for time. It was all very well for Jessie to say they should keep their plans to themselves, but she hadn't reckoned with Onkel Zeb's sharp eyes.

"Ach, I can see as far as the next person. You're different today. And Jessie is, as well."

He'd never been very good at keeping secrets from his uncle. At least he could tell him part of the truth.

"Last night Jessie let me see the letter she got from Alice just before she died. You knew about it, didn't you?"

"Yah, I did." Zeb's face grew sorrowful. "I went to see if she needed anything, and she was just finishing it. I helped her address it and mail it. I didn't know Jessie still had the letter."

"So you don't know what it contained?"

"No. I thought Alice probably wanted to say goodbye to Jessie. They'd always been close."

"She did." Caleb's throat felt rough. "She also said that she'd come back hoping for my forgiveness. And that she hadn't gotten it." He cleared his throat so he could speak. "It made me feel pretty small that she knew I hadn't really forgiven her."

"It's not easy. You know that. It doesn't happen all at once."

"I see that now. The letter opened my eyes to the fact that I've been holding on to my resentment. Reading it…sharing it with Jessie…it seemed as if that set me free. I could forgive…forgive Alice and forgive myself."

Zeb clapped his shoulder, his face working. "Always best to get things out in the open, ain't so?" His voice was husky. "Things heal better that way."

"Yah, they do. I'm out from under a heavy weight. Jessie…" But he'd best be careful what he said about Jessie if he didn't want to give them away.

He saw, through the open window, Jessie hurrying toward the shop. "Here she comes now."

Jessie came in, sweeping the room with a quick glance. "Becky's not here?"

"No. I haven't seen her since breakfast." Caleb's thoughts readjusted. "What's wrong?"

"Ach, nothing," Jessie said quickly, but he saw the little worry line between her brows. "I thought she had gone to gather eggs, but she hasn't come back. Timothy is busy looking for strawberries, and he doesn't know where she is."

"She'll be around here somewhere," Caleb said, vaguely disturbed but not wanting to upset her.

"Most likely she's fallen asleep somewhere," Zeb said. "I mind the time we were looking all over the place for Daniel, and he was up in the hayloft. He'd been hiding from you, and he fell sound asleep."

"That must be it," Jessie said. "I'll have a look around."

"We'll hunt for her, too." Caleb shoved his wheelchair toward the door, his fear mounting.

Jessie hurried ahead as he went out, stopping briefly to talk to Timothy. Reassuring him, most likely.

Common sense told Caleb there was nothing to

worry about. Becky had to be here somewhere. Onkel Zeb was probably right, and she'd fallen asleep.

Reaching the house, he went up the ramp as fast as he could. Jessie would have looked in the house already, but it wouldn't hurt to check again.

He went through the downstairs rooms, calling Becky's name. Nothing. He yanked open the cellar door. There was no logical reason why she'd have gone down there, but he sat at the top and shouted her name. Useless. He was useless, trapped in this chair. He couldn't even go upstairs or down to the cellar in search of his daughter. He shoved the chair to the bottom of the steps leading to the second floor and grasped the newel post. If he could keep hold of the posts, maybe he could pull himself up.

Common sense intervened. Jessie would have looked upstairs first thing. Still, he shouted Becky's name up the steps. No response came.

Back outside again, he could see his son just coming around the corner of the barn from the strawberry patch. Caleb began pushing himself in that direction.

In another moment, Jessie and Onkel Zeb came out of the barn and stood, conferring with each other. Why were they just standing there? Why weren't they hurrying?

Frustration driving him, he tried to move faster, but the chair didn't cooperate on the rough ground. He shoved impatiently and the chair slewed to the side, caught in a rut in the grass. Angry, he yanked at it, overbalancing as he tried to free the wheel. Another angry pull and the whole chair tipped over, spilling him onto the ground.

He had a glimpse of Zeb and Jessie running to help

him as he shoved himself up onto his hands. The cast had taken a jolt, but he didn't think anything was injured. He didn't have time for that now in any event.

Jessie reached him, grasping his arm, but he shoved her away. "Never mind me. Just find my child."

She took a quick step back and then busied herself with righting the chair and holding it steady while Zeb helped him into it, scolding all the time.

"Don't be so foolish. It won't make things better if you get hurt." Zeb settled him in the chair. "Let Timothy help you to the phone shanty in case we need to call for help."

"What are you going to do?" He ignored Jessie, trying to hide the irrational resentment that was building inside him.

"I'm heading up toward the woods. Jessie will go over to Leah and Sam's place."

"If they haven't seen her, I'll ask them to help look," Jessie said as Zeb struck off toward the woods. She put her hand on the chair. "Please, Caleb, go back."

He pushed her hand away. All the darkness he thought he'd banished came storming back, flooding his mind.

"I trusted you with my children. I should have known better."

Jessie whitened. Then she spun and set off for Leah's at a run.

Somehow Jessie managed to keep putting one foot in front of the other as she crossed the field toward Leah's farmhouse. Caleb blamed her. The love he'd shown so briefly was swallowed up in anger at her failure to keep his children safe.

He couldn't blame her more than she blamed herself, though. Her heart twisted in her chest. She had lost Alice. Now she had lost Becky. What kind of person was she, to let down the people she loved?

A failure. She should have taken better care of them. The only thing to do now was pray she could find Becky safe.

Then…then she'd have to go. She'd come here with hopes of doing good, but she'd ended up doing harm. So leaving was her only option.

Please, God, please, God. She prayed in time with her hurrying footsteps. *Please let me find her. Please keep her safe.*

Blinking tears away, she saw Leah coming toward her. Breaking into a run, Jessie reached her.

Before she could speak, Leah had clasped both her hands. "It's all right," she said quickly. "You are looking for Becky, yah?"

Jessie nodded, breathless.

"She's safe. Really." She patted Jessie's hands. "Calm down before you talk to her."

"Yah." She took a breath, thankfulness surging through her. *Thank You, Lord. Thank You.* "Where is she? How did you find her?"

"She's in our barn loft. She's okay. I saw her climbing up. She looked as if she were crying, so I thought it best to say nothing and let you speak to her. Whatever it is, I didn't want to make it worse."

"Denke, Leah. We've been searching everywhere for her. She…she ran off." It was an admission of failure. "Thank the gut Lord she's safe. You're sure she hasn't left?"

"I've been keeping an eye on the barn door. She

hasn't come out. I was just going to send one of the kinder for you when I saw you coming. I'll send him to let Caleb know she's safe."

"Denke," Jessie said again. The word didn't seem enough. "I'll go to her."

"I'll walk with you," Leah said. Gesturing to her oldest boy, she gave him quick instructions as they went.

Jessie felt Leah's gaze on her face as they walked together toward the new barn. She'd have to explain it to Leah later. Now, she must concentrate on the child.

They stopped at the door to the barn, which stood ajar. Leah squeezed her hand in silent encouragement and then turned away. Taking a breath, praying for calm, Jessie walked into the barn.

It was very quiet. The barn was empty of animals at this time of day. Then she heard a small scraping sound from above, and a few fragments of hay drifted down from between the boards of the loft. Becky was almost directly above her.

"Becky," she called. "Where are you?"

Nothing. She imagined Becky freezing, scarcely breathing, like a small animal caught in the beam of a flashlight.

Jessie crossed to the ladder that led to the loft. "Becky, will you come down?"

Again there was no answer. She began to climb, knowing Becky could hear her coming.

When she reached the top she paused. Becky was curled on top of a hay bale against the front wall of the barn, her figure rigid, her face turned away from Jessie.

Relief swept over Jessie at the sight of the child.

She was here. She was safe. The rest could be dealt with, surely.

Walking softly, she crossed to Becky and sat down on the bale next to her. Her prayers reached to God for wisdom, for guidance. When the silence stretched on too long, she spoke softly.

"I'm wonderful glad you're all right, Becky. Daadi was very worried about you."

For a moment there was no response. Then Becky began to cry. "I saw," she said, between sobs. "I saw Daadi kissing you this morning."

"Yah, I thought that must be it." So there had been something to that sound she'd thought she heard this morning. They should have been more careful. This was just what she'd feared—that letting the kinder know about their relationship too soon could ruin everything.

"It made you angry?" she asked.

Becky shook her head, hiccoughing a little. "Not… not angry, exactly. I was…mixed up. Mammi died. Daadi got hurt. Then you came, and I didn't want to like you, but I did. Everything keeps changing." She ended on a wail.

Jessie's heart ached for her. Poor Becky. She was just six. *Everything keeps changing.* How could she understand all the things that had been happening in her short life? It wasn't fair to expect her to.

Jessie could fill in what Becky didn't say. She'd just begun to trust Jessie, and then she'd seen Jessie with her father. No wonder she didn't know what to think. Who could she trust to be there for her?

"I know, Becky. I know." She put her arm around Becky's shoulders, feeling her tremble. But Becky didn't pull away, so Jessie drew the child against her. Sometimes everyone just needed to be held.

They sat in silence for a few moments. Jessie struggled for an answer. For the right words to say. *Gut Lord, guide me*, her heart cried.

She stroked Becky's hair. "It's hard to take so many changes in your life. Not just for you, but for everyone. When your mamm died, I lost someone who was a much-loved little sister to me."

Becky clutched her hand. "She did bad things. Everyone said so."

It sounded as if "everyone" had been careless of what they'd said in front of a small child. "She made mistakes," Jessie said gently. "We can't stop loving someone for making mistakes." She dropped a light kiss on Becky's forehead. "I could never stop loving you no matter what."

Jessie bit her lip. What she'd said was true, but what would Becky think when Jessie left?

She tilted Jessie's face up so that she could see her expression. "Listen to me, Becky. No matter where I go or what I do, I will always love you. And Daadi will always love you…always, always, always. You can be sure of that."

Becky nodded slowly as she struggled to process Jessie's words. She was trying to believe, but her doubts and fears couldn't be cleared up so easily. They were bound to continue, and Jessie's heart seemed to break at knowing she wouldn't be here to help her.

"I think we should go home to Daadi now. What do you think?"

Becky scrambled to her feet. "Daadi. I want to see Daadi."

Together they crossed the loft and climbed down the ladder. They set off. Becky trotted ahead a few steps. Then she stopped, came back and took Jessie's hand. Together they walked toward home.

Caleb saw Becky and Jessie coming toward him across the field. Relief and joy surged through him, closely followed by anger. If Jessie had found her in Sam's barn, why had it taken so long? She should have known he'd be frantic to have his child in his arms again.

He couldn't possibly stay where he was and wait patiently for Becky. He began wheeling himself over the bumpy grass, fighting to keep the chair upright. Zeb came running to grab the wheelchair.

"What are you doing? They're coming. Becky is safe. Do you want to fall again? You won't help matters by getting yourself hurt just when you can see that Becky is fine."

Caleb ground his teeth together, but he had to admit that his uncle was right. It also wouldn't help matters to get into an unseemly tussle with Onkel Zeb over control of the chair.

It seemed to take forever, but it was surely just minutes. When they reached the mowed grass of the yard, Becky let go of Jessie's hand and raced toward him. She flung herself at him, hiding her face in his shirt.

Caleb held her close, murmuring to her. "It's all right. You're here now. It's all right."

He should talk to her about how wrong it had been to run off that way, but not now. Now he just had to hold her and rejoice that no harm had come to her.

Jessie reached them. "Caleb..." Her voice was tentative.

"Not now." He was sharp, but he couldn't help that. He couldn't talk to Jessie without losing what little control he had, so he'd best calm down first.

Regaining his control on that subject took longer than he'd have imagined. Jessie must have realized that, because she went about her usual routine without attempting to speak. The rest of the day passed, and still he hadn't made time to talk to Jessie.

It wasn't until he was lying in bed, staring at the ceiling, that he realized what was really troubling him. Before Jessie came, he'd been...if not happy, at least content with his life. He'd resigned himself to staying single, knowing he could never trust his heart to a woman after Alice. Having Jessie here had shown him how foolish he'd been. He couldn't bar all women from his life because of what Alice had done.

More than that...he couldn't completely blame Alice for what had gone wrong between them. If she'd been too young, too heedless, for marriage, he hadn't been that much better. He hadn't seen the problems for what they were when they began to arise, and he hadn't coped.

But that didn't mean he should fall in love with Jessie. He came back to the source of his anger. He'd trusted her with his children, and look what had happened. The fear he'd felt when he'd realized Becky was missing came surging back.

The sky had begun to lighten along the eastern ridge when he pushed through to what he really felt. He was afraid. Afraid that this love he felt for Jessie wasn't strong enough, afraid that he was jumping into a relationship again, afraid to trust.

You trusted her, one part of him argued. *You trusted her with the kinder, and she let you down.*

She couldn't keep her eyes on them every second of the day, he reminded himself. No one could…and no one should. No kinder could grow up properly if parents protected them that much.

The endless argument was giving him a headache. He had to stop this, had to decide what he was going to say to Jessie. A pang struck him. Jessie must have suffered, too, when she'd seen Becky was gone. She must have told herself that it was just like the day Alice had run off.

He pushed himself upright, sitting on the edge of the bed. Ready or not, the day was beginning. He'd dress, head to the barn, try to be useful. Before he knew it, the van would here to take him to have his cast checked.

Maybe when he returned, he'd have come to some conclusion about what to say to Jessie.

By the time Caleb left for his appointment, Jessie knew what she had to do. She'd waited throughout the early morning for Caleb to speak…to say something, anything, that would tell her what he was feeling.

But he'd said nothing. He'd avoided her eyes and talked to everyone else. She'd failed. And she knew she didn't have any choice.

Leaving the kinder in Onkel Zeb's care, Jessie walked across the field to Leah's house. She found Leah in the kitchen, rolling out pie crust.

"Jessie! What brings you here so early?" Then she

got a glimpse of Jessie's face and dropped the rolling pin. She came quickly to her side, wiping flour from her hands with a tea towel. "What is it? Something has happened. Surely Becky hasn't run off again, has she?"

"No, nothing like that." Jessie hadn't intended to explain anything. She'd thought she'd ask her favor and be on her way. But the sympathy on Leah's face undid her. She blinked back tears. "Caleb blamed me for what happened with Becky. He won't even talk about it."

"You have to make him understand."

She shook her head. "I can't. He won't listen to anything I have to say." She tried to smile, but it was a miserable effort. "Funny, isn't it? Becky ran off because she saw Caleb kiss me."

"You and Caleb…well, all I can say is that it's about time." Leah hugged her. "All the more reason you have to make him listen."

"I tried to talk to him, but in a way he's right. I was responsible for Becky. She was upset enough to run away, and I never saw it."

"Ach, you can't blame yourself for everything. A child Becky's age can be gut at hiding her feelings. And poor Becky's had lots of practice, ain't so?"

Jessie had to admit that was true. Hadn't Becky been convinced that her daadi wouldn't like her if she looked like her mammi?

"There's plenty I could say to Caleb, but it's no use if he can't listen. The only thing is for me to go back home."

"Jessie, no." Leah's arm was around her, comforting her the way Jessie had comforted Becky. "Don't run away."

"I have to." She closed her eyes against the pain. "Please don't argue with me, Leah. Just…help me."

She could almost feel Leah's internal struggle, but finally Leah asked, "What can I do?"

"Will you drive me to the bus? I'll need to leave Zeb with the kinder, and Daniel is at work."

Leah clamped her lips closed. She nodded.

"Gut. Come in about an hour. I'll be packed and ready by then." Jessie made for the door, but not in time to prevent Leah from getting in the last word.

"I'll do it. But I still think you're wrong."

Right or wrong, she didn't have a choice, she told herself as she headed back across the field to the place she now thought of as home. Caleb blamed her. He hadn't trusted her. How could she imagine that they'd be able to build a life together without trust?

Caleb wheeled himself off the lift when the van brought him home again, looking ruefully at the heavy cast still on his leg. His hopes that it might be replaced today were dashed. The technician who worked with him would say only that the doctor would be in touch once he'd received the report. Still, she'd said it with a smile, and Caleb had decided to interpret that as a positive sign.

He waved goodbye to the van driver and turned toward the house. Where was everybody? Usually someone came out when he returned to see if he needed help.

No sooner had he thought it than the door opened

and Becky and Timothy hurtled themselves onto his lap. With a jolt, he saw that they were crying.

"Here, what is it? What's wrong with the two of you? Are you hurt?" He glanced at Onkel Zeb, who'd followed them out, but Zeb was uncharacteristically silent.

"Becky." Caleb pulled her back so that he could see her face. "You must tell me what's happened to cause all these tears."

Becky nodded, gulping. "It's Jessie. Jessie went away. She's gone!" Her words escalated into a wail.

"Jessie left? Where did she go?" He couldn't make sense of this. "What do you mean, she's gone?"

"Leah is taking her to town to catch the bus," Onkel Zeb said. "Jessie said she had to go home." His expression accused Caleb.

Becky cried, "She said she had to go, but..."

Timothy cut off his older sister. "She can't! Who will tell us stories and tuck us in? We need her more than anyone."

"We love her," Becky said. "And she loves us. It's all my fault for running away."

"Hush, now. Nothing's your fault." He tried to grab on to something that might make sense. "Why did you run off, Becky? That's not like you."

Becky sniffled. "'Cause I saw you kissing Jessie. I...I didn't know what to think. I just wanted to be by myself and figure it out."

For a moment he was speechless. "Becky, I didn't know."

"Jessie said you loved me and Timothy more than anything. She said she'd never stop loving us. But now she's going away."

"Daadi will stop her," Timothy declared. "Daadi will bring her home."

"Please, Daadi?" Hope kindled in Becky's eyes.

If Jessie left, he could stop asking himself difficult questions. He could stop dealing with painful truths.

Jessie was loving and honest all the way through. If he blamed her for anything, it was just an excuse not to blame himself.

Hugging his children, he looked at Onkel Zeb. "Will you bring the carriage? We'd best go if we're going to catch them before Jessie gets on the bus."

Zeb broke into a huge grin. Then he trotted toward the barn, shouting at Thomas to help him harness the mare.

They must have harnessed up in record time. In moments they'd brought the family carriage over. With the help of Zeb and Thomas, Caleb hoisted himself up into the seat.

"What are you waiting for?" he said. "Get in."

Still grinning, Zeb helped the young ones into the carriage and climbed in himself. Caleb clucked to the mare, and they were off.

He took the turn onto the road and snapped the lines, urging the mare faster. They'd have to step on it if they were to be in time.

"Faster, Daadi, faster," Becky urged, sliding off the seat to stand behind him. "Hurry."

"I'll go faster, but you sit properly on your seat and hold on. I don't want to lose you."

He'd come close to losing both of them…all wrapped up as he'd been in his own pain. If it hadn't been for Jessie, he might well have done so.

Onkel Zeb had been right all along. Jessie was

probably the only person in the world who could break through to him, because she was hurting just as much as he was. Alice had broken her heart, too. And Jessie had reacted by reaching out to help him despite his rejection.

Once she'd accepted that this was no ordinary, sedate drive, the mare outdid herself, pacing along as if she were pulling a racing sulky instead of a family carriage. Caleb's pulse was pounding in time with the hooves, it seemed. If they didn't make it before Jessie left...

He could write. He could even go out to Ohio after her. But the need to catch her pushed him on. The time for righting wrongs was now, the very minute he realized how wrong he'd been.

They rounded a bend in the road, and the children shouted in excitement.

"There! Leah's buggy. Hurry, Daadi, hurry," Becky said. She was leaning forward as if she could make the buggy go faster.

He closed the gap between the buggies. Surely Leah would hear another buggy behind her, but she didn't slow down. He slapped the reins, the mare put on a burst of speed, and they passed the other buggy. Caleb signaled and pulled slowly to the side of the road, keeping one eye on the mirror to be certain Leah was doing the same. She was, and in a moment both buggies were parked, one behind the other.

Caleb turned, trying to get a look at Jessie's face, but he couldn't. Gritting his teeth, he accepted what he had to do. If only he'd thought to toss the crutches in the buggy before they left.

Swinging his good leg over the step, he lifted the cast, using both hands to move it over, as well.

"Caleb, wait…"

He ignored Onkel Zeb's warning and swung himself outward, grasping the railing with both hands and swinging his legs down. He'd get his feet on the ground, then work his way along the side…

His grip slid, he was losing control, he was falling…

Arms closed around him, supporting him, and he knew without looking that it was Jessie. She held him with both arms clasping him close, so that he could feel her ragged breath.

"What are you trying to do?" she scolded, her voice shaking. "Break the other leg?"

"No." He got one arm around her while he held on to the carriage strut with the other. "Trying to keep you from doing something so foolish as leaving us. Don't you know that we…that I…can't possibly get along without you?"

What else could he say? His thoughts spun frantically. What would show her how much he loved her? What would convince her to stay with them?

She was looking at him, a question in the clear depths of her eyes. "You didn't say anything," she said. "You wouldn't talk to me. How could I know what you were thinking?"

He smoothed his hand down the slender curve of her back. "Ach, Jessie, you should know by now how foolish I am. I had to fight my way through a sleepless night of arguing before I saw the truth for what it is. I love you. Alice's flaws were only human. I forgive her. And I ask God's forgiveness for my mistakes."

Her face softened, warmed. "I'm wonderful glad to hear it."

He found he could breathe again. He wasn't too late. "I'm not done making mistakes myself, you know. I need you, because you keep me straight about who I am. And I love you. For keeps." His heart seemed to be pounding so loudly he couldn't hear anything else. "Please, Jessie. I know you love my kinder. Can you love me, as well?"

She began to smile, and it was like the sun coming out in her face. How had he ever thought her plain? She was the most beautiful sight he'd ever seen. If only she'd speak and say the words that would put him out of his misery. He became aware that the children were hanging out of the carriage over their heads, listening to every word.

Well, why not? This was their future, too.

Jessie's smile encompassed all of them. "I love Becky and Timothy. And I love you, too. All of us belong together."

Caleb's heart was too full for speech. The doubting and anger and bitterness had been a thicket he'd hacked his way through for years, but now the struggling was over. He'd gotten there—to a place of peace and forgiveness.

He could only hold Jessie close and listen to his heart sing with joy. God had taken their broken pieces—his and Jessie's—and fit them together into something wonderful…something that would last a lifetime and beyond.

Epilogue

Spring had come to the valley again. The bulbs Jessie had put in last fall seemed eager to affirm the new life spring brought, sending green leaves unfurling tentatively in the sunshine.

"Mammi, Becky's coming. I see her. Can I run and meet her? Please?" Timothy tugged at her apron, his favorite way of ensuring her attention.

Jessie gave him a quick hug, loving the way it sounded when he and Becky called her Mammi. She looked down the path Becky followed when she walked back and forth to school and spotted her skipping along with Leah's kinder.

"Yah, you can. Mind you stay right with her and don't tease."

Without lingering to respond, Timothy darted across the yard toward the path. Caleb, fixing the pasture fence with Onkel Zeb and Thomas, waved to him and then started toward her.

Jessie walked to meet him, loving the ease with which his lean figure moved now. It had been a long haul, getting his leg back to its normal strength, but he'd made it. Now no one could tell it had ever been injured.

Recovering his strength had meant recovering his confidence, too. Like most men, Caleb could never be content until he could do all the things he expected of himself. He and Onkel Zeb had increased the dairy herd this spring, and with Thomas working full-time, they were able to manage the work among them.

A good thing, too, because Daniel's business had really taken off in the past year. The successful completion of the kitchen project he'd done for the Englischers had brought him as much business as he could handle, and he had taken on two apprentices to work alongside him.

Now, if only Daniel could find a good woman...

Caleb reached her and put his arm around her for a quick hug. "What are you thinking about, looking so serious?"

"How happy we are," she said, returning his hug. "And how I wish Daniel would find someone to love."

"Don't go making matches," Caleb warned. "He'll fall in love one day, and that will be it for him. You'll see. After all, it happened for us, ain't so?"

She nodded, wondering if he'd ever realized that she'd loved him since that first day when he'd come to her parents' farm. "Yah, and just when everyone was giving up on you."

He smiled. "It wasn't everyone's business. Just yours and mine."

"And Becky's and Timothy's," Jessie reminded him.

"Them, too," he agreed. He pressed his hand lightly against her rounding belly. "And this little one's."

Jessie put her hand over his, love overflowing her

heart. "I never thought to be as happy as I am right now."

He held her closer. "Me, also. God has given us the gifts we didn't even know to ask for."

Contentment flooded through her. Caleb was right. Even when they hadn't known what was best for them, God had known. He had seen them through the pain and brought them to this joy, and she was forever grateful.

* * * * *

If you enjoyed
SECOND CHANCE AMISH BRIDE,
be sure to pick up
AMISH CHRISTMAS BLESSINGS
from Love Inspired,
featuring Marta Perry's
THE MIDWIFE'S CHRISTMAS SURPRISE

Find more great reads at www.LoveInspired.com

Dear Reader,

Thank you so much for deciding to read my latest story. I hope you enjoyed reading it as much as I did creating it!

I have always been touched by the importance with which the Amish view forgiveness. Their firm belief that they will be forgiven in the same measure they forgive others is at the bedrock of faith.

That doesn't mean it is easier for the Amish than it is for any other Christian. All of us must surely struggle with forgiving the wrongs that have been done to us and to our loved ones. Sometimes I think I must forgive the same things over and over again, every day, until at last I realize that the forgiveness sticks!

Caleb and Jessie struggle with this concept of forgiveness in my story, and it doesn't come easy for either of them. I hope you were moved by their struggles, and you feel they'd earned their happy ending when they finally succeeded.

I'd love to hear what you think of my story. You can contact me at my website, www.martaperry.com, find me on Facebook, www.facebook.com/MartaPerryBooks, or write to me at marta@martaperry.com or in care of Love Inspired Books, 195 Broadway, 24th Fl, New York, NY 10007. I'll be happy to send you a signed bookmark and my brochure of Pennsylvania Dutch recipes.

Blessings,
Marta Perry

COMING NEXT MONTH FROM
Love Inspired®

Available September 19, 2017

AMISH CHRISTMAS TWINS
Christmas Twins • by Patricia Davids
After returning to her Amish community, pregnant widow and mom of twins
Willa Chase is devastated when her grandfather turns her away. An accident
strands her at the home of John Miller—jolting the reclusive widower out of
sorrow and into a Christmas full of joy and hope for a second chance at family.

THE RANCHER'S MISTLETOE BRIDE
Wyoming Cowboys • by Jill Kemerer
Managing Lexi Harrington's newly inherited ranch through the holidays might
not have been cowboy Clint Romine's brightest idea. Getting close to her
means revealing secrets he's long kept hidden. And falling for her means he'll
have to convince Lexi her home isn't back in the big city—but in his arms.

AN ALASKAN CHRISTMAS
Alaskan Grooms • by Belle Calhoune
Single mom Maggie Richards is ready to embrace a new future in Love,
Alaska—restoring the gift shop she's inherited in time for Christmas. But she
gets a blast from the past when childhood pal Finn O'Rourke offers help. With
both of them working together, will love become the most unexpected holiday
gift of all?

MOUNTAIN COUNTRY COWBOY
Hearts of Hunter Ridge • by Glynna Kaye
For cowboy Cash Herrera, taking a job at Hunter's Hideaway ranch is a chance
to gain custody of his son—and work for lovely Rio Hunter. Rio knows the secret
she's keeping means leaving Hunter Ridge, but spending time with Cash and
his little boy has her wishing for a home with the man who's claiming her heart.

MENDING THE WIDOW'S HEART
Liberty Creek • by Mia Ross
From her first meeting with Sam Calhoun, military widow and single mom
Holly Andrews feels a surprising kinship. But she's not looking for permanence.
Working on a youth baseball league together rekindles dreams Sam had all but
abandoned. Can he convince Holly to stay in Liberty Creek, with him, forever?

A BABY FOR THE DOCTOR
Family Blessings • by Stephanie Dees
Jordan Conley knows Dr. Ash Sheehan would be a perfect pediatrician for
her new foster son—but her heart-pounding crush on the confirmed bachelor
complicates things. Besides, she's horses and hay, and he's fancy suits. But
the more involved he gets in their lives, the more she wishes they could stay
together...always.

_____

**LOOK FOR THESE AND OTHER LOVE INSPIRED BOOKS WHEREVER
BOOKS ARE SOLD, INCLUDING MOST BOOKSTORES, SUPERMARKETS,
DISCOUNT STORES AND DRUGSTORES.**

LICNM0917

Get 2 Free Books,
Plus 2 Free Gifts—
just for trying the
Reader Service!

SPECIAL EXCERPT FROM

Love Inspired®

When an accident strands pregnant widow Willa Chase and her twins at the home of John Miller, she doesn't know if she'll make it back to her Amish community for Christmas. But the reclusive widower soon finds himself hoping for a second chance at family.

Read on for a sneak peek of
AMISH CHRISTMAS TWINS by USA TODAY
bestselling author **Patricia Davids***,*
the first in the three-book **CHRISTMAS TWINS** *series.*

John waited beside Samuel's sleigh and tried unsuccessfully to curb his excitement. He was almost as giddy as Megan and Lucy. A sleigh ride with Willa at his side was his idea of the perfect winter evening, especially since he didn't have to drive. Lucy was the first one out of the house. She quickly claimed her spot in the front seat beside Samuel. Megan came out next and scrambled up beside her sister. He'd never seen the twins so delighted.

Willa took John's hand as he helped her in. He gave her gloved fingers a quick squeeze and saw her smile before she looked down.

Samuel slapped the lines and the big horse took off down the snow-covered lane. Sleigh bells jingled merrily in time with the horse's footfalls, and Megan and Lucy tried to catch snowflakes on their tongues between giggles.

John leaned down to see Willa's face. "Are you warm

enough?" She nodded, but her cheeks looked rosy and cold. John took off his woolen scarf and wrapped it around her head to cover her mouth and nose.

"Danki," she murmured.

"Don't mention it. In spite of the cold, it's a lovely evening to go caroling, isn't it?" The thick snow obscured the horizon and made it feel as if they were riding inside a glass snow globe. The fields lay hidden under a thick blanket of white. A hushed stillness filled the air, broken only by the jingle of the harness bells and the muffled thudding of the horse's feet.

Their first destination was only a mile from John's house. As Lucy and Megan scrambled down from the sleigh, John offered Willa his hand to help her out.

"Was this what you imagined Christmas would be like when you decided to return to your Amish family?"

She shook her head. "I never imagined anything like this. Do you do it every year?"

"We do."

"You aren't going to actually sing, are you, John?"

He threw back his head and laughed. "*Nee*, but I will hum along."

"Softly, dear, softly," she suggested.

He wondered if she realized that she had called him "dear." It was turning out to be an even more wonderful night than he had hoped for.

Don't miss
AMISH CHRISTMAS TWINS
by Patricia Davids, available October 2017 wherever
Love Inspired® books and ebooks are sold.

www.LoveInspired.com